The damned tentacle shot up again. Only that time it was followed by two more appendages and the entirety of the beast's head. His mouth burst open, and millions of flies emerged, swarming around me, getting in my eyes and my hair and my ears and my face. I swatted at them, ducked my head, and tried to run—tried even harder not to be grossed out—but the truth was, I wasn't fast enough. The bugs did their job, and as I tried to shove through the dense, living mass, I felt something thick and cold lash itself around my ankle.

As Rose screamed, I rolled over, slashing at the tentacle, half-terrified that I'd miss and get my leg, and the other half of me not caring if I lost all my limbs so long as I got free.

It wasn't any use.

Penemue was dragging me back toward hell.

TURNED

BOOK THREE IN THE
BLOOD LILY CHRONICLES

JULIE KENNER

ACE BOOKS, NEW YORK

THE BERKLEY PUBLISHING GROUP
Published by the Penguin Group
Penguin Group (USA) Inc.
375 Hudson Street, New York, New York 10014, USA
Penguin Group (Canada), 90 Eglinton Avenue East, Suite 700, Toronto, Ontario M4P 2Y3, Canada
(a division of Pearson Penguin Canada Inc.)
Penguin Books Ltd., 80 Strand, London WC2R 0RL, England
Penguin Group Ireland, 25 St. Stephen's Green, Dublin 2, Ireland (a division of Penguin Books Ltd.)
Penguin Group (Australia), 250 Camberwell Road, Camberwell, Victoria 3124, Australia
(a division of Pearson Australia Group Pty. Ltd.)
Penguin Books India Pvt. Ltd., 11 Community Centre, Panchsheel Park, New Delhi—110 017, India
Penguin Group (NZ), 67 Apollo Drive, Rosedale, North Shore 0632, New Zealand
(a division of Pearson New Zealand Ltd.)
Penguin Books (South Africa) (Pty.) Ltd., 24 Sturdee Avenue, Rosebank, Johannesburg 2196,
South Africa

Penguin Books Ltd., Registered Offices: 80 Strand, London WC2R 0RL, England

TURNED

An Ace Book / published by arrangement with the author

PRINTING HISTORY
Ace mass-market edition / January 2010

Copyright © 2010 by Julie Kenner.
Cover art by Craig White.
Cover design by Annette Fiore DeFex.
Interior text design by Laura K. Corless.

ISBN: 978-0-441-01811-6

ACE
Ace Books are published by The Berkley Publishing Group,
a division of Penguin Group (USA) Inc.,
375 Hudson Street, New York, New York 10014.
ACE and the "A" design are trademarks of Penguin Group (USA) Inc.

PRINTED IN THE UNITED STATES OF AMERICA

10 9 8 7 6 5 4 3 2 1

To my friends, my family, and my fans.
Thanks!

ONE

My name is Lily Carlyle, and because of me, the world is counting down to the Apocalypse.

How would you like that on *your* résumé?

Trust me when I say it sucks.

Not that I did it on purpose, mind you. I was tricked. Told I was keeping the demons out when really I was making sure they each had a front-row seat to the end of humanity.

And we're not talking some namby-pamby Internet countdown by some hoo-ha who read Revelation, heard about an earthquake in Taiwan, and concluded that The End Is Nigh.

No, I'm talking the full-meal deal. The real end of the world. When the demonic horsemen are going to burst from the demon realm to swarm over the earth like a plague of really nasty locusts, feeding off torture and torment and evil and lies.

Not a happy time. Trust me on that.

It's coming because of me. I can say that. I can accept it.

But that's not the end of the story. Like every good player, I've got a card up my sleeve. Two, actually.

Play the Ace of Spades, and I can use the *Oris Clef*, a demonic key that I tracked down, stealing it from a master demon who'd been determined to find it. It won't lock the gate closed, but it will lock it open. And every demon who crosses over owes fealty to the one who wields that key. I'd be a queen, the most powerful creature on earth.

Except I'd be a demon queen, thrust into power by a demonic tool. And the demonic essence that lives inside me—that I've been trying so hard to suppress and compartmentalize and control so that I could hang on to humanity by my fingernails—would surely rise up. It's hard enough fighting it as things are. Fighting it when that kind of power is at stake?

Honestly, I didn't think I could control the madness. I'd make a hell of earth whether I wanted to or not, and a demon of myself. So far, my track record has been less than stellar. I'd tried to avenge my sister and gotten killed instead. I'd tried to stop the Apocalypse, then nailed the gates open. Not really a vote of confidence in my ability to be a warm, fuzzy demon queen. I was pretty sure I'd lose it. I'd give in to the dark. I'd become horrible and vile and dangerous even if I didn't want to.

And then we have door number two. Play the Ace of Hearts, and I can actually lock the Ninth Gate shut tight. Because it turns out there is at least one way left that will do that. Trouble is, that lock is me. *My* body. *My* blood. All I have to do is toss myself into the hell dimension right as the portal opens.

No problem, you say? Kill yourself. Go to heaven. Accept the afterlife accolades that would surely come with stopping Armageddon.

Um, don't I wish?

Because I can't die. Not even if you whack off my head. I'd still be alive. In pieces, sure, but alive.

Alive, and suffering. My flesh burning forever. An eternity of agony and horror and utter torment. Torture beyond endurance with absolutely no escape.

Dear God in heaven, "scared" doesn't even begin to describe it.

I've read the bio of Joan of Arc, and yeah, I want to be like her. But then I look at what I am and who I am, and the truth is I'm not St. Joan material. I'm terrified of the pain. Petrified by the torment. And when I peer into hell like that, I've got to admit that the demon-queen thing looks better and better.

But the one thing worse than suffering in the fires of hell is letting down the entire planet. Which pretty much sums up my dilemma.

As you can tell, I'm not sure which way I'm going to go, because both options suck big-time.

But the end is rushing fast toward all of us.

And soon, I'm going to have to make a choice. I hope like hell I make the right one . . .

two

"Run!"

Deacon's voice cut through the haze in my head, and I realized that the ground was shaking, huge chunks of concrete and lethally sharp steel girders thrusting upward as the earth buckled and snapped.

Except this wasn't an earthquake. This was much, much worse.

I didn't argue, didn't stop to analyze. Instead, I grabbed my sister's hand and tugged her across the undulating floor of Zane's fast-disintegrating training basement. There was only one way out, and we needed to be on that elevator. Right then. Right that very second.

Because I knew what was under the floor—I hadn't seen it, but I was certain.

Penemue. A master demon.

More specifically, a master demon I'd just royally screwed. Somehow, I had a feeling he wasn't planning a nice, reasonable little chat. Instead, he wanted what hung around my neck: the *Oris Clef*. The key that would lock open the Ninth Gate to Hell and give the bearer dominion over all the demons who crossed into the earthly realm.

"Lily!" Rose's shriek was filled with terror, and I turned automatically in the direction she was looking: Behind us, the floor had opened like a sick parody of a flower, concrete peeling away like inelegant petals to reveal a deep pit that reached all the way down into the blackest depths of hell.

"Move." I grabbed her arm and wrenched her back into motion even as I visually scoured the dust and rubble for Deacon.

The stench of sulphur filled my nostrils as the chasm burped vomit green gas. From the black pit in the ground, I could hear a deep, menacing rumbling as what was down there began to emerge—the demon himself in all his powerful, festering, massive glory.

And beyond him, separated from me and Rose by the widening void and the rising beast, I saw Deacon.

"Go!" he shouted. "Just *go.*"

One long, squidlike tentacle shot free of the abyss, then crashed down, shattering the ground as if it were no more substantial than Styrofoam.

"Dammit, Lily! Run!"

I knew I should. Knew I needed to get the hell out of there. But I couldn't. Instead, I stood stock-still, my hand on my knife, my jaw clenched. *This* was the beast who had fucked up my life. This was the beast who had pulled the strings to trick me and make me believe I'd been doing good when really I'd been Evil's puppet.

This was the bastard who'd done that to me, and damned if I didn't want to look in his eyes. Damned if I didn't want to ram my blade right through him. And, yeah, I wanted to wallow in the darkness that filled me following a demon kill, the bitter black that was the price I paid for doing what I was created to do. A master demon like Penemue would be the ultimate hit, beyond anything I'd experienced before. And oh, yeah, like an addict, I craved what could so easily destroy me. But I didn't care. I wanted it. Hell, I *needed* it.

"Lily!" Rose screamed as the tentacle lashed out toward us, coming so close we could feel the breeze left in its wake. She screamed again, the sharp edge of her fear cutting through both my fury and my craving. I took a step backward, abandoning my demonicidal fantasies.

Because the truth was, I couldn't end him. Not this beast. Not even with all the power that came from being Prophecy Girl.

He was too much—too massive, too powerful. And even with my supercharged body and über-girl skills, I was no match for him. I couldn't risk losing. Not to him. Not then.

Lose, and he would get the *Oris Clef*.

Lose, and he would use it.

Lose, and Penemue would control all of the demons that crossed over at the convergence. He'd rule the Horsemen of the Apocalypse. Not four, but four billion. Even more. Countless, untold demons that would cover the earth like a plague. And Penemue the master of them all.

Not if I could help it. With Rose's scream still echoing in my ear, I turned, grabbed her hand, and ran, the floor buckling beneath our feet as we fled across the room.

"Lily!" Rose tripped over a length of steel girder rising from the concrete like a sentinel. She slammed to the ground, crying out in pain as the sharp edges of stone and metal sliced through her jeans and cut into her hands.

No time to worry about that, though. I grabbed the back of her T-shirt and hauled her to her feet. "Go!" I shouted. She stumbled a bit, probably not entirely used to her new legs and taller body, but to her credit, she picked up speed and headed toward the elevator, not falling despite the way the floor was undulating beneath her.

"Come on, come on! Dammit, come on!" Rose tugged on the gate to the old-fashioned elevator, trying to slide it aside, but it was easy enough to see that her efforts were futile. A little fact that sucked big-time, because as far as I knew, there was no other way out of the basement that had once been Zane's prison.

I clenched my jaw, determined not to die. Not when Zane had sacrificed himself, banking on me to step up to save the whole damn world. I feared I didn't have it in me to be the hero that the world needed, but right then I didn't have to find out. Right then, all I had to do was survive.

I pushed in beside Rose and grabbed hold, then gave the gate a good, solid tug.

Nothing.

Well, damn. What was the point of superstrength if you couldn't even open one stuck door?

I spun around, searching for Deacon. I needed his help, but he was still yards away, circumventing the gulch that was opening wider and wider in the floor, sucking everything in—furniture, weapons, training ring—as if it were a black hole. I held my breath because Deacon had lost his left hand, so he had only one set of fingers with which to grip the wall. The gray-metal cabinet was still bolted there, and as I watched, Deacon ripped open the door one-handed, then pulled out a crossbow. He met my eyes, then tossed the weapon toward me.

Penemue's tentacle lashed out blindly, knocking the crossbow off its trajectory, but I launched myself sideways and managed to catch it before it disappeared into the abyss. Deacon pitched a quiver of arrows next, and those I caught more easily, then quickly slid the sheath onto my back and hefted the crossbow, already feeling better for the weapon in my hand. My knife was the only thing that would actually kill a demon once and for all, but under the circumstances, I was keen on just knowing I could slow the creature down. Although I have to say, a crossbow wasn't exactly a panacea. Considering the size of the beast fighting its way up through the concrete floor, what I really needed was a missile launcher.

Deacon armed himself, too, then grabbed onto the

door and used it to swing himself over the edge of the widening chasm. I held my breath. There were only about three inches of floor left where he was. If he tripped . . . If he needed to reach out and grab something . . .

But he didn't, and once his feet were on firm ground I allowed myself one tense breath. He was steady, but he was hardly safe yet. He stood with his back pressed to the wall, his toes hanging over the ragged concrete edge in a sick parody of a suicidal jumper balancing on a high-rise ledge.

"Deacon! Hurry!" I shouted, as he pushed away from the wall and leaped from the narrow portion to where the ground widened. He landed, steady, and I exhaled in relief, only to feel the sharp sting of cold horror as the tentacle lashed out, circled his waist, and pulled him backward into the abyss.

"No!" I yelled, as Rose cried out Deacon's name.

I don't remember moving, but I was on my belly, my hand reaching out, down into the blackness. Down into where Deacon had gone. Into the night, into the void, into hell.

"Deacon!" I screamed, though I could see nothing in the dark. Not him. Not Penemue. Not even the fires of hell. "Deacon!" I cried. "Deacon! Can you hear me?"

But even as I called, I knew it was futile. He was lost, and my stomach roiled as I choked back bile, willing myself to keep focused and in control despite the fact that my demonic partner had been thrust back into the hell that he'd so desperately longed to escape.

I couldn't think about that just then. If anything, Deacon had bought us time, and I was going to use it. No way was his getting sucked down into hell going to mean the end of me and my sister.

"Come on," I said, scooting back from the abyss and grabbing Rose's elbow. She stood stock-still, her face pale, her lips parted as if she wanted to say something but couldn't quite find the words. "Rose!" I snapped, tugging her back toward the elevator. "Move."

Not that my determination got us any farther. Deacon's demise hadn't magically loosened the elevator gate, and we were still down in the training basement, trapped beside a hole to hell where a gigantic demon would surely reemerge at any moment.

Fuck.

I gave the gate one more futile yank, then kicked the damn thing. It was no ordinary metal we were dealing with. As a training arena for preternatural assassins, the room was chock-full of special protections. How nice.

"Can you make a portal?" Rose asked. "Can you get us out of here?"

I closed my eyes and concentrated, but nothing happened. I'd only recently acquired the skill to create a "bridge" that would take me and my companions through space, time, and the whole nine yards. I'd done it just a few minutes ago, actually, when Rose, Deacon, and I had been racing for our lives. But we'd been returning from a quest for a mystical vessel, and without some object as my goal, I didn't have any way to mentally anchor the bridge.

Which was the long, rambling way of saying that we were stuck.

"We'll figure something out," I said, giving the gate another hard yank.

"Lily . . ." Her voice was low, and far too steady. Which to me meant that she was scared shitless.

I looked over my shoulder—and immediately saw why. A mountainous mass was rising from the dark, like the time-lapse formation of primeval hills. The purple mountains majesty, however, weren't covered with demon slime, and the viscous, snotlike goo that slathered this demonic head made me want to puke.

It wasn't like I hadn't seen scaly, slimy demons before, but the Grykon I'd fought my first day on the job had been more or less my size. A monster, sure, but still manageable.

This, though . . .

The head alone was the size of a Suburban even without the massive, filth-covered horns that extended at least five feet in opposite directions.

His eyes were red with black slits for pupils, and, within the black, I swear I could see the souls of the damned. He had no nose, only what appeared to be a rotting orifice, and green slime oozed out. His skin looked to be as tough as an elephant's hide, and it appeared to be moving, as if living things were sliding around under the flesh.

"Lily . . ." Beside me, Rose whimpered.

"Don't look," I said, pushing her behind me as I

lifted the crossbow that seemed utterly insubstantial. "Don't look; don't watch. We'll be fine."

I reached up and closed my hand around the necklace that was the *Oris Clef*, the demonic key that Penemue himself had created and I'd recovered only moments before. The thing had the power to control the coming apocalyptic horde of demons, and damned if I didn't wish I had that power right then. At the moment, a subservient hell monster would be a really good thing.

"What are we going to do?" Rose said.

"Defend ourselves," I said. I raised my crossbow. "Ourselves, and the *Oris Clef*."

So far, our only advantage was that Penemue had slowed down. At first, the building had been crumbling around us. But when Deacon had disappeared, so had the demon's tentacles. He'd returned, but his ascent was so slow that I had to wonder if he was half-in and half-out of some other dimension.

"You need to go," Rose said. "Pick something, use your arm, and just *go*."

I kept my eye firmly on the crossbow's sight. "One, it's not that simple. Two, I'm not leaving you." I'd cozied up to hell—literally—to save my sister, and there was no way I was going to throw her to the wolves. Or the demons.

A long wail filled the room, and we both stared at the gaping hole that was the demon's rising mouth. His eyes were like fire, and his tentacle thrust up, then slammed back down again only a few feet from us, rendering bits of broken concrete into dust.

"Shit!" I cried, bracing my body against the useless elevator. "Something's going on. There's no way he should have missed us."

Something *was* going on, and my heart lifted a little when I realized what it had to be: *Deacon*. He was down there fighting. Buying us time.

He was giving us a gift, and we damn well needed to use it.

"I'm going to check the weapons cabinet," I said.

"Right now?" Her voice was high, squeaky, and terrified.

I didn't expect to find anything to kill Penemue with, but maybe I'd find something to help me open the elevator. For that matter, if I could get to Zane's office, maybe he had some sort of override button. I didn't know. All I could think about was not wasting the chance that Deacon was giving us.

"He'll catch you!" Rose said, as I started in that direction. "He'll knock you in!"

"I'll be careful," I said, but even as I spoke, the tentacle burst free, along with the shoulders of the beast, making the floor buckle and tossing me onto my ass. Penemue lashed out, and it was clear he was aiming right for me. I fired, the arrow shooting true—embedding itself right into that slimy, sickening skull.

Fabulous, I thought. And then amended the thought to *Holy freaking shit*, because my arrow was ejected immediately, thrust out of the demon's flesh by the intense force of a horrific column of fire.

I threw myself sideways, missing the bulk of the blast, but it still scorched my jeans.

"Lily!" Rose called.

"I'm okay!" I held on to the crossbow as I scooted along the floor, abandoning my plan to head to the cabinet. Instead, I had a better idea.

"Get down," I shouted, then raced toward the elevator, the crossbow aimed at Penemue. "The ground, Rose! On the ground!" The tentacle swiveled and turned, and I dodged it. The head had disappeared beneath floor level, but I needed to see it again, and I took a chance and yelled for Deacon. "Let him go! I have an idea!"

I heard a low rumble like an oncoming earthquake, so deep and menacing it made my insides tremble. And then the demon burst up, the slime-covered head breaching the shattered floor, as if someone holding him down had suddenly let go and the beast had been overwhelmed by his own velocity.

I aimed. I fired.

And as soon as the arrow was free, I threw myself to the ground, barely missing the burst of fire that shot from Penemue's punctured skull. The blast shot over both me and Rose, slamming exactly where I'd hoped—right in the middle of the elevator gate.

Bingo.

The gate didn't open, but it didn't matter because now there was a giant hole in the metal mesh.

"In," I shouted to Rose. "Get in!"

Rose didn't need my encouragement. She was already climbing through the hole and calling for me to follow her. I didn't have to be told twice, and I scrambled in that direction, over a floor that was buckling and moving again beneath my feet as the beast surged up, pissed off and determined to stop me.

The damned tentacle shot up again. Only that time it was followed by two more appendages and the entirety of the beast's head. His mouth burst open, and millions of flies emerged, swarming around me, getting in my eyes and my hair and my ears and my face. I swatted at them, ducked my head, and tried to run—tried even harder not to be grossed out—but the truth was, I wasn't fast enough. The bugs did their job, and as I tried to shove through the dense, living mass, I felt something thick and cold lash itself around my ankle.

As Rose screamed, I rolled over, slashing at the tentacle, half-terrified that I'd miss and get my leg, and the other half of me not caring if I lost all my limbs so long as I got free.

It wasn't any use.

Penemue was dragging me back toward hell.

I reached down, grabbing onto the tentacle and trying to pry it off with my fingers. As I did, I looked up, and found myself staring into the demon's face. Into its eyes.

Oh, fuck.

I felt the snap—the sharp tug when I was pulled into another creature's thoughts. Another little gift of mine, and one that I really didn't welcome at the moment, but I had no choice, because I was in and the horror was around me, the fires and the pain and, oh God, my skin—my skin was burning, the flesh curling, turning to ash as I watched, as I suffered and cried, then starting all over again, the pain so intense I swear it was alive, and I couldn't do anything except scream and scream and scream and—

Snap!

The connection broke. I'd shut my eyes in terror, the reflex freeing me from the horror. A horror, I knew, that would be mine if I did what needed to be done. If I played the martyr. If I stepped up and saved the world.

I breathed deep, trying to control my trembling.

Dear God, how could I ever find the courage?

"Lily!"

Rose's voice cut through my fear and self-loathing, and I reminded myself that I didn't need that courage now. Now I just needed to get out of there.

With a fresh burst of determination, I rolled to my side as the tentacle tugged on my leg, this time thrusting my knife into the ground and trying with all my might to halt our progress toward the abyss. I slammed it down hard, shoving it into a crevice in the concrete, then closing my hand tight around it. With my free hand, I grabbed a protruding metal beam, my muscles straining as I tried to pull myself up.

"Nothing's happening!" Rose called. "The buttons don't work!"

Okay, I confess I wasn't completely interested in the

state of the elevator at the moment, although I did want my sister to get out of there. Pretty soon, I figured she was going to have plenty of time to escape. Because once the demon had me and the key, it really wasn't going to give a flip about her.

But the other thing I was afraid of was that the demon would realize that she was the way to get to me. Take her hostage, and I was going to be Cooperation Girl. I knew it, and so, I feared, did the demon.

My fears were borne home when the pressure of the tentacle around my leg let up, and I screamed out in both anger and fear as the appendage lashed forward to close around Rose's waist.

She howled, using her knife to hack uselessly at the tentacle that refused to let go. I rushed forward to join her, thrusting my blade in and twisting, but the demon's tentacle seemed immune to pain.

"It's getting tighter! Lily, oh God, make it stop!"

I stabbed my knife down deep into the spongy flesh, and started sawing, wishing the blade was serrated, because I was damn well going to saw through all fifteen inches of flesh if that was what it took.

But I had to saw fast, because she was struggling, her mouth open, her breath coming in gasps, and fear pounding behind her eyes.

I was going to lose her. *Oh God, oh God.* I was going to lose her. Rose. My little sister. The little girl I'd risked everything—including the Apocalypse—to save.

I felt numb. I felt raw. And I felt wholly and completely impotent.

And then, as her eyes began to dim and I could barely see the dent I was making in the demon's flesh from the tears floating in my eyes, I heard it.

Low at first, then building up strength. A deep, terrifying wail.

I turned, saw the demon's eyes go wide, the black shifting to red. I turned back fast, and acting solely on instinct I grabbed Rose around the waist, then spread my legs, my feet anchored inside the elevator, one foot on either side of the hole that had been blasted in the cage door.

It was the right move. The tentacle pulled back, retreating, and trying to take Rose with it.

But it couldn't. Not easily, anyway. Not with me holding on to her.

And damned if it didn't let go.

I didn't completely understand why. All I knew was that whatever had produced that horrific wailing noise had scared Penemue. And he'd retreated into the darkness.

I figured it would be a good idea to get out of there, too. Because even in my limited experience in this world, I'd already figured out that it's a good idea to run from things that disturb massive beasts from hell.

I slapped Rose's face, heard her moan, and sighed with relief. I didn't have time to do more, though. So I let go and let her fall to the floor of the elevator car. She coughed, and rolled over, and I knew that for the moment at least, she was safe.

I jabbed at the elevator buttons, but Rose was right—

they didn't work. We needed out of there, though, and I tilted my head back, searching for the emergency door that was standard in all elevators. Including, apparently, those installed by minions of hell.

I used the broken metal of the cage as a makeshift ladder and managed to get up there, then pulled the trapdoor down. Then I hopped back down and made a stirrup with my hands for Rose to step in. "Can you manage?"

She lifted her head, looking a lot like a girl who badly needed a nap.

"Rose, please. We've got to move."

She opened her mouth, but no sound came out. To her credit, though, she did stand. As she did, her eyes darted toward the hole in the elevator door and out toward the chasm. I knew what she was thinking, because I was thinking the same thing: *Unless I'm dead or broken, I'm getting the hell out of here.*

I held out a hand to steady her as she came over, then re-formed the stirrup for her. "Grab my shoulders," I said.

"I'm okay." Her voice was weak, but she meant what she said, and even before I had time to worry if she'd have the strength in her arms to pull herself up, she was through the hole, and I saw her peering down, waiting for me to join her.

I was just about to do that very thing when the tentacle thrust toward me again. I leaped, trying to get through the trapdoor. Rose grabbed the back of my shirt and tugged, trying to help me up, but it wasn't enough. Despite my strength and her valiant effort, the tug of the tentacle that had lashed around my waist kept me from climbing through the escape hatch.

It would have pulled me all the way back to hell with it, if it wasn't for a coal black, winged creature that burst from the gorge. It shot forward as if fired from a cannon, flame dancing over its body, not as if it were on fire, but as if it *was* fire.

And the fire-creature roared straight for us, the flames dissipating as it grabbed me under my arms, then shot straight up into the elevator shaft, effectively pulling my lower body free of the tentacle, which had loosened only slightly, as if shocked to see the creature.

It slowed enough to grab Rose with its other arm, then it put on a fresh burst of speed and rocketed straight up, up, up—at least until we jerked to a stop, flipped over, and started moving in the opposite direction. In other words, back *toward* Penemue. Which really wasn't where I wanted to go.

I called out in protest, but it was no use. Penemue was down there, two floors below, and we were heading right for him. The demon's bulbous body filled the elevator shaft, that black pit of a mouth sucking us in, as if we were the very air he needed to breathe. As if we were caught in some damned sci-fi tractor beam, and we were moving backward, toward the gaping maw.

I screamed and struggled in my captor's arms, desperate to get me and Rose out of there. A reaction that was, of course, idiotic, because if I got free, gravity would send me hurtling down into Penemue's waiting mouth. And once that little fact registered in my head, I clung more tightly to my winged rescuer. I didn't know who he was or what he wanted, but at least until he got us out of the elevator shaft, he was my new best friend.

And right then, my friend was fighting dirty.

He thrust his torso and legs up, so that his head was pointed down, and Rose and I were pulled in close to his side. And then, as I watched, he let out a wail that came straight from the deepest pit of hell and emitted a burst of flame from his mouth so hot that I had to close my eyes and twist my face away. But when it dissipated, I turned back, then sucked in air at what I saw— the entire elevator shaft had melted away, and Penemue had retreated, leaving one burned-off tentacle behind, the flames still snapping at the crispy flesh.

"He will be back." The low voice rumbled through me, rough and inhuman and yet also somehow familiar. My breath caught, and warm fear flowed through me as my mind filled with horrible possibilities.

I had no time to ponder those fears, though. Not then. Not as he shifted direction in the shaft, and we began shooting upward, so fast I feared that we'd slam into the masonry and die from massive hematomas.

Not that I had to worry about that. As we approached at breakneck speed, our savior released another burst of flame and melted the floor above us, along with the ceiling above. Handy trick, that.

We burst out into the dead of night, rising high above the city, all of Boarhurst before us and the lights of Boston proper twinkling in the distance.

He dropped down then, and, as my heart pounded in my chest, the beast landed us softly on a patch of grass, his arms releasing us as he stepped back, wings folded, head down, crouched there in front of us.

Beside me, Rose was breathing in and out fast as she scrabbled backward, crablike, away from him.

Me, I stayed put, holding tight to my knife.

But I didn't attack. I knew this creature. I was certain of it.

And when he lifted his head, I saw it in his eyes.

"Deacon?"

Something dark flashed in those eyes, and he lunged, teeth bared, mouth open as if another burst of flame was coming.

Rose screamed, and I tackled her to the ground, then rolled over and thrust out my knife, wondering what the hell use it could possibly be against a demon who could breathe fire as Deacon did.

"Go," he said, his muscles practically trembling with restraint.

I didn't. I just stood there, awed and shaken and—yes—more than a little freaked-out.

"Go," he repeated. "Find the last key. Find it," he growled, "before it's too late."

THREE

"What did he mean by that?" Rose asked, not nearly as winded as I'd expect after running so far. Apparently she was getting the benefit of Kiera's fabulously fit body. "'The last key'?"

We were in a park several miles from where Deacon had dumped us, having raced away before Deacon lost control of his inner demon and decided to bite our heads off.

I grimaced, the mental sarcasm I so often fell back on in a crisis feeling heavy and wrong. Because the only reason Deacon was in a stereotypical demonic form now was because of me—because he'd given up his own chance at redemption in order to save me. If he'd given me up, he'd still be the man, not the beast, and guilt settled over me, heavy and cloying.

I squeezed my eyes shut, remembering what had happened right before we'd ended up in that basement with Penemue. We'd been trapped in a chamber, and Gabriel had found me there. The archangel had been dogging my steps for a while, and this time, when he finally captured me, he also explained why: I was a key, too. I could lock the gate and keep the demonic hordes at bay. All I had to do was tumble into hell when the convergence came.

All I had to do was suffer forever in the fiery pit.

And Gabriel intended for me to do exactly that.

When Deacon made it clear that he wasn't down with Gabriel's sacrifice-Lily plan, the angel promised him redemption—the very thing that Deacon had sought so hard, the promise that had given him the courage and resolve to claw his way up from hell and keep him on a path that totally defied his own nature.

But despite being offered exactly what he had strived for, Deacon had said no. Because of me.

Because he believed that he and I could find a way to close the gate together and save both our souls.

He'd given up everything he'd been fighting for, then paid the ultimate price.

"Lily?" Rose's voice was as soft as the gentle touch of her hand on my arm. "Lily, what did he mean?"

"What he's always talked about," I said. "That there's still one key out there. One key that can lock the Ninth Gate shut tight and prevent the demons from coming across."

She licked her lips, then shifted on the ground, wincing as she did so. I frowned, leaning in to look at the nasty cut on her leg. "Do you think he's right?"

"I don't know," I said. "Hold still." I'd sheathed my knife in the holster on my thigh, so I pulled it out and sliced the tip of my finger. Rose's eyes went wide.

"A gift from Zane," I said, referring to my former trainer. A long story, but because of him, my blood had the power to heal. At least, I assumed it did. I hadn't yet successfully taken that particular skill for a test-drive on someone else.

I traced my bloody finger along the slash in Rose's thigh, then breathed a sigh of relief when the flesh started to knit in its wake.

"Wow," Rose said, and I had to agree. "But the key. You really think Deacon's right?"

I didn't know. My fear was that he *had* been right—but that the mysterious missing key had been found: me.

That would suck, because the idea of a third key was something that had my heart dancing in an excited little rumba rhythm. Because if there was a key, that meant that if I found it, I could pick door number three: Use the key, stop the Apocalypse. Forget sacrificing myself or putting on the black crown of demonic royalty. I'd have an easy out.

And honestly, as crazy as my life had been since I'd died, *easy* sounded pretty damned appealing.

"So how do we find out?"

I stood up, dusting off my jeans. "Deacon," I said.

Her brows rose. "The same Deacon who looked like he wanted to bite off our heads?"

"That's the one. The convergence is coming. Whatever progress he's made looking for the key saves us time." And besides, I wanted to see him again. Wanted to tell him I understood what he had done for me, and that the sacrifice meant more to me than I could ever possibly express. And, yeah, I wanted to try to get back the Deacon I knew. The Deacon who'd slipped inside my heart and given me the courage to keep fighting the dark.

"So, what?" Rose said. "We go to his house? Do you even know where his house is?"

"No," I said. "But you were there. And so was—oh, shit! Rachel!"

"Huh? What about Rachel?"

"We left her at Deacon's."

Rachel was my sister. Or, rather, Rachel was Alice's sister. And since the demons had sacrificed Alice so that they could shove my soul into her body and fulfill some fucked-up prophecy, that meant that I was now Alice. Or some sort of Alice-Lily hybrid.

Honestly, it's all very confusing.

The bottom line is that before Rose, Deacon, and I had headed off to fight the big, bad demon, Deacon had tucked Rachel away safe and sound in his house. At the time, it had made sense—he'd been one of the good guys.

Now, though . . .

Now Rachel was hanging out in a house owned by a demon who'd returned to his demonic form and had hellfire for breath.

"Rachel's in his house," I said, spelling it out for my little sister. "She doesn't know Deacon's changed."

Rose's eyes went wide as the import of my words registered. "Oh, no."

"Yeah," I said. "Definitely an *oh, no* situation."

I knew there was still humanity left inside Deacon—he'd told us to run, right? But I had no idea how hard the demonic part of him was struggling to prevail. Probably pretty damn hard. After all, before he betrayed his fellow demons in an attempt to earn his way into heaven, Deacon had been among the worst of the worst. A Tri-Jal demon, tortured in the deepest, darkest depths of hell until any vestige of self had slipped away.

But he'd managed to fight. Managed to shove down the demonic part of himself. And that's not an easy task. Believe me, I know.

Every time I kill a demon with my own blade, I not only absorb the demon's strength; I also absorb some of its essence.

Which meant that I knew how Deacon felt with a demonic presence rising inside him, begging to get out, seizing on any opportunity to gain a toehold in the real world.

Once the demon's out, it's hard to shove him back into the bottle, and I was desperately afraid that was a battle that Deacon would lose. Worse, I feared that Rachel was about to come face-to-face with a Deacon-demon.

"What should we do?" Rose asked.

"Don't you know where Deacon's house is?" Like Rachel, Rose had once hidden in Deacon's home, safely ensconced while he and I fought the threat on the street.

I, however, hadn't thought to tag along when he had taken them home. I hadn't even scribbled down a street address.

"No idea," Rose said. "But it wasn't too far away. And it was big. And old. Like in one of those fancy neighborhoods."

"Would you recognize it if you saw it again?"

She shrugged, looking fourteen despite the twenty-something body. "Dunno."

I frowned, frustrated. What was I supposed to do? Drive down every street in every nice neighborhood in the Greater Boston area? At the moment, my fantabu-lous Rand McNally arm was seeming like a big, use-less nothing. "We need to find someone who can find people." My arm could locate objects, but people—and demons—were beyond its capabilities.

"Like a private detective?"

"I was thinking more along the lines of a psychic."

Her brows lifted. "A psychic? Puh-lease."

I couldn't help it—I laughed. "We're both running around in new bodies," I said, counting my comments off on my fingers. "We just escaped from a demon the size of a small house. My arm can create a mystical map, then send me all the way to other side of the world in the blink of an eye. And I can steal the thoughts from your head simply by touching you and looking into your eyes. But you're leery about a psychic?"

"Well, you know," she said with a casual lift of her shoulder. "It just sounds so whoo-woo."

I shook my head. *Unbelievable.*

"Besides," she added. "Do you even know any psychics?"

"Remember your tattoo?" When she'd first come to stay with me, I'd wanted to mark her as Rose, primarily because at the time there was a hideous, horrible, vile demon camped out inside her body. I'd taken her to see a tattoo artist I knew, and while he did his work on Rose, I chatted up the psychic who had space in his front parlor. Madame Parrish. A woman with a lot more going on than met the eye.

Rose squinted at me, clearly confused.

"Trust me," I said, then tilted my head toward the street. "Come on."

"We're walking?" Her voice rose with incredulity. "To the flats?"

I didn't even bother looking at her. Instead, I was checking out the cars parked along the road. What I really wanted was my motorcycle, but I'd left my vintage Tiger back at my apartment.

"Oh," Rose said, catching on. She pointed at a stylish convertible parked on the far side of the road in front of a row of high-priced condos. "How about that one?"

Tempting, but I went for an old Buick instead. Less conspicuous. Easier, more accessible wiring.

In my previous life (the one I lived as Lily Carlyle in Lily Carlyle's body), I'd done some not-so-aboveboard things. Like, oh, stealing a few cars. And even though I'd always returned them, I'd also always felt slightly guilty about my lapses into such felonious activity.

Now, though, I was grateful I'd had such a wide range of experiences.

I wasn't wearing a watch, so I didn't know what time it was, but no one was on the streets. Rose found a heavy rock, and I forced myself not to insist that she look the other way as I broke in and hot-wired the car. This was her life now, too. For better or for worse.

So far, I have to say, my little sister was definitely experiencing the "worse" side of the equation.

The clock on our stolen ride's dash said that it was just after 2:00 A.M., but I wasn't worried about the late hour, as I'd caught up with Madame Parrish in the wee hours several times before. I guess it made sense, really. Psychics probably did their best business after the bars closed and everyone who hadn't gotten lucky wanted to know when their turn was coming.

The ride to the flats was uneventful, which was great, as the possibility for havoc was endless: angry demons, pissed-off angels, the cops trying to nail me for Grand Theft Auto.

I left the Buick on a side street, then the two of us started walking the six blocks to the tattoo parlor.

"Hey," Rose said as we passed a twenty-four-hour convenience store. "Did you see this?"

She'd come to a halt in front of a battered blue newspaper machine, and I backtracked to her side. EARTHQUAKE, blared the headline, which went on to announce that hundreds were dead and thousands injured after a 7.6 earthquake hit Shanghai.

"Holy crap," I said. "Seven-point-six is huge."

"I know," Rose said, her face pale as she tilted her head to look at me. "But did you see the date?"

"Of the earthquake?" I turned back to skim the lead paragraph.

"Of the paper."

I glanced up at the masthead, then took an involuntary step backward. "That's not possible."

"Yeah," she said. "I know. But either someone is pulling a really huge joke, or we skipped over a huge chunk of time when we went into the portal."

She spoke reasonably, as if she were discussing a math proof with her geometry teacher. Apparently the idea of losing days and days didn't bother her in the same way that going to visit a psychic did.

It bothered me, though. It bothered me a lot. Not only because it's just downright freaky to lose time like that, but also because the convergence was coming with the next full moon. And unless I was very mistaken, *that* was now coming in less than a week.

"Fuck," I said, then rummaged in the pockets of my once-pristine but now-battered red duster for some change. Naturally, I had nothing. "Quarters?"

Rose checked the pockets of her denim jacket, then checked her jeans. "Nope." I frowned, then jerked hard on the pull-down door of the machine. The metal protested, then snapped, and the door fell open. I reached in, snagged the paper, and started walking fast down the street, Rose right beside me. "What are you looking for?"

"Weather," I said, passing her the sections that didn't

interest me. "Sunrise, sunset, moon phases. That stuff." I flipped pages, then finally found what I was looking for. I stopped walking long enough to skim the text, then cursed when what I read confirmed my fears. "Five days," I said. "The next full moon is in exactly five days."

"Five days?" Her voice rose with incredulity. "But—but—we're supposed to have almost two weeks."

"Not anymore," I said grimly.

"Holy crap," she said, and I shared the sentiment. "So, like, when exactly? Dawn? Sunset? The middle of rush hour?"

That, I thought, was a really good question. And right then, I really wished Deacon was around to help me figure out the answer.

"Clarence said the portal between us and the hell dimension is opening over Boston, and he said it would happen at the next full moon."

"Right. I know. Do you still trust him?"

Considering that Clarence had been my frog-faced demonic handler—Penemue's right-hand man, the demon who'd lied to me about pretty much every little thing—it was a legitimate question. "About this, yes. He didn't have any reason to lie about time and place."

"So? That still doesn't tell us exactly when. Or exactly where."

"I'm guessing moonrise," I said. I skimmed the paper. "That's 12:04 in the afternoon. Practically shaves a whole day off the time frame."

"The afternoon?" Rose said, her voice rising. "How can the moon rise in the afternoon?"

"It just . . ." I waved a hand, trying to remember high school astronomy. "It just can."

"What if you're wrong?"

"I'm not," I said, trying to sound more confident than I felt. "And I'll figure out a way to double-check."

"And where?" she asked, hurrying to catch up as I started walking again.

"Give it a rest, Rose," I snapped, because I needed answers *right then*, and I didn't have them, and that pretty much sucked. "We'll figure it out."

Thank goodness I no longer needed sleep. I sure as hell no longer had time for it.

Despite the late hour, the street was bright, the fluorescent and neon signs of the bodegas, cafés, porn stores, and tattoo parlors casting a synthetic glow over the grimy street. We were only about two blocks away from our destination, and I picked up the pace, anxious to arrive. I had no particular fear or concern, yet I wanted off the street. I felt edgy and anxious, like a heroin addict jonesing for a hit, and I peered into the shadows as we moved, my gaze searching for creatures that didn't belong. Demons. Beasties I could kill to satisfy the death lust that was welling so forcefully within me.

I tried to shake off the urge, focusing instead on Madame Parrish. We were almost there, and I stepped up my pace in anticipation of sitting and talking with her. She was an odd creature who had managed to pluck some of my secrets right out of my head, yet it had never occurred to me not to trust her. That probably made me naïve, but there was something about her that reminded me of my mother. Or, at least, of *a* mother. It was a feeling I liked, and one that could only survive on a diet of trust and faith. Analyze the emotion, and I would find no basis, and in that fleeting moment, that sense of safety I felt in her presence would disappear forever.

I wasn't sure what that said about her or about me. But I was certain that I needed to see her. If for no other reason than that I needed to feel the blanket of comfort settle once again around my shoulders.

As we crossed the street for the final block's walk, a squat man in faded army fatigues fell in step beside us. "It's coming," he said, his soft voice contrasting his grizzled appearance.

I stopped and peered at him more closely. Rose stopped, too, and her hand pressed into my shoulder as she stood behind me. I could feel her breath on my neck and knew that she was also peering suspiciously at this stranger.

"What's coming?" I asked, sliding my hand down to grasp the hilt of my knife. The motion pushed my duster back, revealing the thigh holster and the blade, but I didn't care. Right then, I was more than happy to advertise the fact that I was armed, and then some.

His mouth stretched into a wide, mirthless grin. "The end," he said, tapping my paper. "Earthquakes. Hunger. Devastation. It begins," he said. "It has begun." I started walking again, but he fell into step beside us. "Are you ready?" he asked. "Are you ready for the end times? Repent," he said, finally stopping as we picked up speed. "Repent, repent, repent."

I don't know why he creeped me out so much—after all, he was right. But he did, and by the time we reached the middle of the block, my heart was pounding in my chest, and Rose's hand was clutched tight in mine.

"He's right, isn't he?" Rose said. "It's coming."

I tilted my head to the side, cracking my neck. "Not if I can help it."

She stayed silent, and I turned sideways, surprised to find her eyes welling with tears. "If we don't find the third key . . ." she said, then trailed off, and I knew she was remembering what the archangel Gabriel said about how my blood and my body could stop this nightmare from happening. For everyone, that is, except me.

"Rose?"

She sniffed, then spoke to the sidewalk as she tugged me to a stop beside her. "I don't want you to leave me."

"I don't either," I said. "We'll find it."

She lifted her head, and I saw that her eyes were rimmed in red. "What if we don't?"

I closed my eyes and drew in a breath. She hadn't asked, but I heard the underlying question: Will you do it? Will you die to save us?

I didn't answer. How could I when I didn't know what to say? I'd done all this stuff to save my sister, and unless I found that third key or plunked on the demon-queen hat, she wouldn't be truly safe unless I burned in hell forever. I'd come so far, and yet I wasn't sure I could take that final step. Because I knew what it meant—I'd seen it through Penemue's eyes. I'd *felt* it. And that reality had been a billion times worse than even my most vivid nightmares of hell.

"I'm scared, Lily," she said, voicing my thoughts.

"Me, too." I reached out and squeezed her hand. I'd sacrificed so much already to keep Rose safe, and I'd done it without fear or remorse. I'd even gone out to kill a man, knowing I was committing a most grievous sin and might not survive the effort.

I'd been prepared to burn in hell for my actions, but to be truly honest, I'm not so sure I'd believed in either heaven or hell back then. Just living and dead. And if I was dead, then it was over. Blackness. Nothingness. And although the idea of the dark had terrified me as a child, when you got right down to it, how scary could nothing be?

But I finally understood. Hell existed, all right. It was pain and torment and maddening torture. It was childhood nightmares on crack and torture porn movies come to life. It was horror beyond imagining.

Even for Rose, I wasn't sure I could make the sacrifice. Not after what I'd seen, what I'd felt.

I didn't want to have to acknowledge my own weakness, much less try to conquer it, yet time was counting down. I had five days left. Five days to find another way.

Five measly days to find Deacon and the key that he'd so firmly believed existed.

The door to the tattoo parlor stood propped open by an old-fashioned canister-style ashtray that had either been used a lot that night or never emptied. The handwritten *Madame Parrish, Psychic* sign was propped in the window, and I released a small sigh of relief. Finally, something was going right.

We stepped through the door to find the place going strong, despite the late hour. At least a half dozen people were hanging out in the lobby paging through John's sample books, looking for the perfect logo with which to annotate their bodies.

Rose eyed the screen behind which John was working on his current customer, her teeth scraping her lower lip. "Should I do it again?"

I hesitated, not sure how to answer. Before, I'd wanted Rose to have something solid—something tangible—to remind her of who she was at the core, no matter what hideous demonic hitchhikers happened to have come along for the ride.

And Rose's hitchhiker had been pretty damn bad: Lucas Johnson was the man who'd stalked and raped her, who'd brutalized and beaten her. A man the system had been unable to corral.

A man who'd turned out to be a demon.

We'd managed to get him out of her body, but the cost had been huge—she'd had to give up the body she'd had for fourteen years. And if she wanted to get herself another tattoo now that she was living in a different body, I was hardly going to say no.

"Do you want to?"

Her lips pursed, and she looked incredibly young and innocent despite being in Kiera's body. She had a battle-scarred look about her and an angular face that was full of attitude, accentuated by vivid pink hair. Not really the look I'd ever expected for my beautiful sister, but I had to admit she carried it well. She looked like she could take care of herself. So far, that was only an illusion. But at least it was an illusion that made me feel better.

Her face relaxed, and she shook her head. "No," she said, then met my eyes. "I know who I am. I don't need a tattoo to remind me."

Rock on, little sister.

I hooked an arm around her shoulder. "Come on, then."

We skirted the group checking out the tattoo images, then stopped in front of a curtained-off section. I tapped lightly on the wall, hoping that Madame wasn't with a client, and was greeted by her soft voice telling me to come on in. I pushed the curtain aside, and Rose and I stepped in, leaving the fluorescent intensity of John's area for the homey comfort of Madame Parrish's corner of the world.

I saw her immediately, her small, wizened body swallowed by a floral-print armchair. She looked up, her eyes soft, then put the book she was reading down in her lap and held out her free hand to me. "Lily," she said. "Child, it is very good to see you."

"You, too."

"And Rose." She held out her hand for my sister,

then tilted her head to the side. "Do not worry, little one. You have a warrior's body now. Soon enough, you will have a warrior's heart to go with it."

I licked my lips and forced myself to stay quiet. The truth was, Rose might be in a demon assassin's body, but that didn't mean I wanted her stepping up to the demon-killing plate. I liked to believe that in a pinch, Kiera's body would take care of her, but I didn't want her getting into the pinch in the first place. This was my little sister—the one I was supposed to protect. And I wasn't keen on tossing her into the fire.

Rose, though, had apparently been thinking along more warrior-oriented lines. A little fact that made me frown.

Madame Parrish laughed. "Her life is complicated, Lily, but it is hers. You must give her the freedom to live it. To fight alongside you if need be."

"I'll take it under advisement," I said. I knew that despite her gifts, Madame Parrish could no longer get inside my head—I'd managed to block anyone from doing that. But Rose was an open book to her. And as for me . . . Well, just because my thoughts were my own didn't mean that the crafty psychic didn't have common sense. She could read my moods well enough even without any psychic hoo-doo.

"Are you practicing?" she asked me.

"Practicing?"

"Seeing, without letting the seen know that you are there?"

"Ah." I cleared my throat. I have the ability—inherited

from Alice—to get inside people's heads. It happens when I look into their eyes while touching them, and it's a little bit freaky. Thoughts and images all jumbled up. But it's useful, too, especially for the sneaking-around and figuring-things-out part of my new life.

The only problem is that the person whose head I'm in knows that I'm in there. Which means that *stealth* isn't part of the equation.

I'd asked Madame to help me fix that little problem. Her prescription? Practice.

Oh, joy.

"I've gotten some practice in," I admitted, which was true. But I wasn't all the way up to stealth yet. "I've been a little busy."

"Don't back off from the practice," she said. "There will come a time when you will be pleased you have gained this skill."

"Oh." I licked my lips, wondering what she knew that I didn't. "Uh, why?"

But she just smiled.

I cleared my throat. "Right. Well. Anyway, that's not why we're here."

"Of course not," she said, gesturing to the small couch. "You are afraid you have lost someone."

Beside me, Rose leaned forward eagerly. "You know where he is?"

Madame shook her head at the question, but her eyes never left me. "I don't."

"But—"

She leaned forward, putting her hand on mine and

effectively silencing my question. "Sometimes, things lost can find their way back home again."

I leaned back, letting that settle in my head.

"You mean—?" Rose began, then silenced herself when Madame pressed a finger to her lips.

"I am sorry, girls. I don't believe I have much help to offer you today."

She'd helped enough, though. At least I knew that Deacon could come back. That one more time, he might win the battle that raged inside him.

I hoped he believed in himself enough. More than that, I hoped he won soon. Because I needed his help.

I started to push myself up off the couch, then stopped, the weight of another question pressing me back down. At the end of the world, it was all on my shoulders, and I wanted to know why. "Why me?"

Her smile was gentle. "Does there have to be a reason?"

"No," I admitted. "But I think there usually is. The world's a big place, you know. With a lot of people. And out of all of the billions, how come I'm the one who's stuck fighting demons and saving the world? How come I'm the one who has to make impossible choices?"

"We all fight in our own ways," Madame said, making me feel a bit like an arrogant heel. "But I do understand your question." Her eyes cut to Rose. "What do you think, child? Why has your sister been handed this burden?"

"Me?" Rose squeaked. "I don't know. Why on earth would I know?"

Madame's brows lifted, and for a second I had the feeling that she wanted to argue, which made no sense. If I had no clue why me, then why on earth would Madame think that Rose had a clue?

Then Madame Parrish smiled and held out her hand for Rose. "It's all right, child," she said. She shifted her smile to me. "As I said, there does not always have to be a reason. And sometimes, it takes a while for the reason to appear."

Another cryptic response. Honestly, I probably should be used to them by now.

I stood to go, signaling for Rose to do the same. "I know you won't tell me how you know the things you know," I began. "But—"

I cut myself off, realizing I was about to ask one of those Big Questions that aren't supposed to be voiced.

She took a sip of tea, then looked up at me. For a moment, my vision faltered, because she appeared to be other than herself. Her face no longer looked fragile. In fact, I had the odd sensation that it was marked—tribal tats fading in around intense black eyes. A face so familiar and yet—

Gabriel.

I stumbled backward, realizing I was seeing—imagining?—the archangel Gabriel's face superimposed over Madame Parrish's face.

But as soon as I made the connection, the illusion faded, and I was looking only at the psychic, her eyes tired and her own familiar face as lined and fragile as crumpled tissue paper. "I don't know," she said.

I held my breath, almost scared to speak. "What don't you know?"

"How this will all turn out."

I nodded, confused and unreasonably disappointed. I licked my lips. "I saw— Are you—?"

"But I do know that I have faith," she said, ignoring my stammered question. "In the future, Lily, and in the choice that you must make."

FOUR

"So where to now?" Rose asked, curling up in the corner of the Oldsmobile we were traveling in. I'd left the Buick in the alley, figuring we'd be safer in a different vehicle. Not that I was overwhelmingly worried about the police, but time was running out, and I really didn't need the hassle.

"The Bloody Tongue," I said, referring to the pub in which I, as Alice, now owned a half interest along with Rachel. Rose needed to sleep, and I needed to think, and I was no longer concerned about Rachel. After all, it had been over a week since Deacon and Rose and I had disappeared, and my worry that Rachel was still in Deacon's house had faded. Rachel's no doormat, and when no one came back in a reasonable time, she would have left, plain and simple.

And that meant that she'd be at her own condo or the pub. Considering the late hour, I guessed she was at home asleep, and I intended to take advantage of the apartment above the pub and tuck Rose in to do the same.

We'd catch Rachel when she came into work the next morning; and then we could all figure out what to do next, my primary goal being to find Deacon so that we could find that key.

Rose nodded, then pulled her feet up onto the bench seat and rested her chin on her knees. She closed her eyes and catnapped as I steered the car onto the highway, trying to remember how to get from the flats back to Boarhurst. "So what did Madame Parrish mean?" Rose asked, about the time I was peering at exit signs.

I glanced sideways. "I thought you were asleep."

She shrugged. "Can't."

"You need to try." I might not need sleep anymore, but she did. Or, at least, I assumed she did. With her in Kiera's body, I wasn't entirely sure about the rules anymore.

And, honestly, even if she didn't *have* to sleep, I didn't feel like I was doing my part as a responsible big sister unless I at least made her try.

"I tried. I dozed. Now I'm awake. And you're avoiding my question."

I sighed. "What was the question?"

It was her turn to sigh, loud and put-upon. "I asked what she meant. About having faith in you." A single tear trickled down her cheek. "Is she talking about what Gabriel said? That you have to get tossed in? To hell, I mean?"

I shook my head. "Absolutely not. She was just talking. Like a pregame pep talk."

"But—"

"We have to have faith," I said. "Plain and simple." Faith that I'd find another key, or that I'd have the strength to do what needed to be done and not give in to the chocolate-dark pull of the demon within.

I reached up to finger the *Oris Clef*. I wasn't sure I could do that. More, I wasn't sure I had Madame's faith. The darkness in me loomed up when I least expected it, and I feared that one day I would no longer have the strength to fight it. That it would consume me as it had already consumed Deacon, and the Lily I wanted to be would be gone, replaced by something vile. Something hateful and demonic and dark.

We drove in silence for a while as I maneuvered the streets of Boarhurst, finally parking the car two streets over from the pub.

"We should just take the T," Rose said. "I mean, it sucks for the people whose cars you keep stealing."

"If I manage to save the world, we can consider it part of my fee. And if I screw it up, I think one stolen car is going to be the least of their worries."

She made a face, then shoved her hands in the pockets of her jacket. "You're so touchy."

"Imagine that," I said, though I knew she was right. I didn't want to be touchy, but I really couldn't help it.

"Yeesh," she said, then moved two steps ahead of me. I hurried to catch up, telling myself that I was just being smart and careful rather than legitimately concerned. But as my gaze took in the deep shadows cast between the low, thick buildings, I had to admit that the truth leaned much more toward the concerned side.

"Rose," I whispered, my hand going to my knife and my eyes trying to peer deep into the shadows. "Slow up."

To her credit, she immediately shifted from petulant teenager to wary warrior. "What?" she asked, and I saw with approval that her own knife was already drawn.

"Maybe nothing," I admitted. "But I have a bad feeling."

Her lips pressed together, and her forehead furrowed. It was, I realized, an utterly Rose expression.

"So what do we do?"

"Keep going," I said. "But be watchful."

That, it turned out, was utterly useless advice, because "keep going" was an impossible directive, as our way was suddenly barred by the two humongous men in serious need of dental work who'd eased out of the shadows in front of us.

"Well, well," one of them said. "Looky what we got."

I stepped forward, protecting my sister. She moved closer, her hand on my shoulder.

"Get out of my way," I said, wishing I had Kiera's nose. She could smell demons. Me, I just smelled their BO.

"Rose?" I asked. "Are they?"

"How the heck should I know? They look mean enough."

One of them chuckled, low and menacing. "Mean? Nah, we ain't mean. We're gonna be damn nice to you ladies. Just you wait and see how nice we are."

"Thanks," I said, drawing my blade. "But I'm going to decline your gracious invitation."

I couldn't see behind me, but I could hear, and what I heard was motion that didn't sound like Rose, especially since she was standing stock-still, the tightness of her fingers telegraphing her fear.

I watched our two harassers' faces and saw the tell-tale flicker in the shorter one's eye as he looked up, and the tiny nod of his head as permission was granted.

Oh no, you don't either.

I spun around, pushing Rose down as I aimed, then let my knife fly. It landed hard in the chest of the man who'd been sneaking up behind us, his own knife drawn.

Or, to be more accurate, the *demon* who'd been sneaking up. I'd gambled, and it had paid off, because the beast I'd nailed was melting into a pile of black goo, and I could feel the hit of demonic essence and strength that filled me whenever I took a demon out, that lovely little side bennie of being Prophecy Girl.

I whipped back around, yanking the switchblade from my back pocket as I moved. I saw the hesitation flicker in the bigger one's eyes, and I stepped forward, smiling. "That's right, buddy," I said. "You picked the wrong girl to mess with."

"You are not worthy to wield it," the second one said, sneering at the *Oris Clef* around my neck as Rose scampered forward and pushed the blade that she'd recovered into my free hand.

"No? You think you are?" I smiled, slow and confident. Because *this* was what I wanted. What I'd wanted since Penemue. He might be too much for me to take on, but those guys? I could take those guys. I'd take them. I'd kill them. And when their essences oozed out, I'd soak them up and revel in the dark.

Hell, yes.

"Just try it," I whispered.

Dude number one apparently had some iota of intelligence, because he actually took a step away from me. But no way was I getting harassed by two demons on the street and letting them escape. That simply wasn't happening, and he must have figured it out, because he stopped heading backward and instead put on a burst of speed and rushed forward toward Rose, even as Number Two rushed me, whipping a sword out of a hidden sheath on his back and swinging it at me so fast and violently that I couldn't get any velocity going with my knife.

"Lily!"

"Run!" I cried, as Number Two thrust again with the sword. I couldn't turn around to help Rose, not without risking having my head removed from my body, and so I determined instead to bring this battle to a speedy conclusion. A slow dance with the vile beast might have been more satisfying—it certainly would have fed the darkness that was writhing within me—but I needed to wrap this up and help my sister.

He came at me again, leading with his sword, and I thrust my hand up and blocked it with my knife. Or tried to, anyway. The demon was damn strong, and my knife went clattering into the street. The sword came at me again, polished metal glinting in the streetlights. I did the first thing I could think of—instead of retreating as would be expected, I ran straight toward the fast-moving blade, then clapped my hands tight over the steel. I held it there, the muscles in my arms straining as he tried to thrust it forward and impale me.

As he did, he moved closer to me—too close. And I kicked out, hard and fast, right in his shriveled demon nuts.

The anatomy might not always be the same, but in his case it was close enough. He yowled, and as he did, his hold on the sword relaxed just enough for me to shift my hands, grab the blade, and pull.

I yanked it free, then spun it around, shifting my grip to the hilt and lashing out at him, all in one fluid motion that would have made my demonic trainers proud. I got him in the neck, and the blade sliced through skin, muscles, bone, and tendons, sending his head flying into the street.

He wasn't dead, though, not really. In order to kill a demon so that he can't come back, he has to be killed with a blade the wielder has made his or her own—in other words, a blade that has spilled its wielder's blood. The sword never cut me, so I dove for my own knife, then slammed the point into the barrel chest of demon Number Two.

Immediately, the black goo started to flow, and as it did, I tilted my head back, sucking in the essence. He was dark, that one, and I trembled from the power he'd possessed, thick and rich like maple syrup.

"Bitch!" The voice rang behind me, and it wasn't directed at me. I turned to find Rose holding her own, Kiera's speed and strength working to her advantage. But she didn't have Kiera's instincts or timing yet, and she wasn't going to survive much longer.

"Hey! Ugly!"

To his credit, the demon responded to his name, and when he turned, I let my blade fly. It lodged in his throat, the wound not sufficient to kill. Rose, however, didn't waste a moment. She yanked the blade out, then plunged it back in again, this time, right into the vile beast's heart.

The demon dropped to the ground, a bubble of black demon blood forming at its mouth.

"Shouldn't he melt?" she asked. I took the blade, pulled it from his heart, then plunged it in one more time.

"Yeah," I said, as the body started to ooze away—as the essence roiled through me. "He should."

We stood there for a moment, breathing hard. Rose simply catching her breath, and me riding the high of the kill, sucking in the darkness that, I knew, gave me too much of a dark thrill.

I was like an addict, wanting the power of the hit. But how much more power would there be if I was the demon queen? I reached up and fingered the *Oris Clef*.

I could almost feel it gathering power as the convergence drew near, and I couldn't help but think of what it offered me. And of what I would be so horribly foolish to take. I could barely control the essence that surged through me after a kill. The power that came with being queen? I didn't think I could handle *that* at all.

"Wow," Rose said, her eyes on the dissolving body.

"Wow," I agreed.

We started walking toward the pub.

"So, I did good, right? I mean, I'm alive, and I stabbed him and everything."

I frowned at the idea of "good" and "I stabbed him" coexisting in my sister's personal universe. But as I bent down to pick up the sheath and sword, I had to acknowledge that she was right. I squeezed her hand. "You did great."

She grinned, completely proud and practically humming with energy. I couldn't help it—I pulled her close and hugged her.

"What?" she said, hugging me back before wriggling free.

"Nothing," I said. "Just glad we're both safe." But it was more than that. I thought back to the way she used to look. The paper shell that had been my sister. There was life in her now, like there had been before Lucas Johnson, and that was worth all the hell I'd been through.

"What now?" she asked, as we finally reached the back door to the pub.

"Now you sleep."

"No way!" she protested, as I rummaged in my pocket for the key. "I mean, it's the end of the world. Shouldn't we sleep later?"

"*You* need to sleep," I said, biting back a laugh. "And *I* need to think."

"Whatever." Frustrated, she popped a beer bottle with her toes. It went flying down the alley and disappeared into a shadow. I expected we'd hear the sharp sound of shattering glass. Instead, a low, guttural, "What the fuck?" echoed back toward us.

Immediately, I drew my blade. "Who's there?" I demanded. "Show yourself."

Nothing.

Behind me, I heard Rose's soft breathing. "What is it?" she whispered.

I shook my head, trying to hear who or what was in the alley with us.

"Give me your knife," I whispered. She did, pressing it into my waiting hand after I switched my own blade to my left hand. I closed my palm around the hilt, testing its weight, familiarizing myself with the weapon. And then I fixed my gaze on my target, hauled back, and let the blade fly.

The weapon whipped forward, tumbling hilt over blade, to disappear into the shadows in front of us. A split second later, a sharp yowl reached my ears, and a skinny, red-haired creature slumped out of the shadow, his hands closed over the hilt of Rose's blade, which was now lodged firmly in his thigh.

"Forgive!" he yelled, his voice a deep baritone that

contrasted with his skinny-kid appearance. "Forgive, mistress! Forgive!"

I looked at Rose, who'd edged up beside me to get a better look. *Mistress?*

"Who the hell are you?" I asked, my own blade back in my right hand.

"Morwain, mistress," the creature said.

"You human?"

Morwain shook his head. "Demon, mistress. Your servant, mistress."

"Servant?" Rose asked, not the least bit scared. Neither was I, for that matter. I'd met some nasty, scary demons in my life. Morwain was not one of them.

Then again, I thought, raising my knife again, *appearances could be deceiving.*

"I serve the queen," Morwain said, his eyes remaining on me as he dropped to one knee, not breaking his gaze until he bent his head in supplication.

O-kay.

"I'm not your queen," I said, even though it was probably stupid to argue with a demon who was holding back from attacking me because he had delusions about the extent of my authority.

"Perhaps not yet, mistress," he said, reaching up to touch his own neck. "But soon, mistress. Soon."

Ah. Well, wasn't that special?

I thought about what I'd seen inside Gabriel's head as I'd fought to escape him. Millions of demons down on their knees, each pledging to serve their queen—*me*.

The vision had come hard and fast: the demons

crossing over, and me standing at the gate, the *Oris Clef* clutched tight between my hands.

I hadn't actually heard what I'd said in the vision, but I knew the sound track even so. *By the power of my blood, I claim my destiny as the leader of those who would pass.* And then I'd slit my palm with my blade and pressed it hard against the filigree-encapsuled gemstone that I wore around my neck.

I shivered, hating the fact that the image was almost as tempting as it was disgusting. Hating that even though I loathed the demonic essence inside of me, still I craved more. Craved that ultimate hit that would come from the *Oris Clef*'s power. But the part that was still me? I knew I wouldn't be able to control it, no matter how much the demon in me whispered otherwise.

"I'm not your queen," I said firmly to Morwain, then pulled my blade. "I'm not, and I won't ever be."

"But, mistress."

I took a step toward him, leading with the knife. He was a demon, and I killed demons. It was what I was. What I did. And right then, it was what I wanted.

He backed away, the picture of contrition. "I have offended thee, mistress. Forgive. Forgive."

Screw that. I took a step toward him, ready to fight, ready to kill, then stopped as Rose's hand closed over my arm. "Don't," she said simply.

I turned to her, aghast. "He's a demon, in case you've forgotten what the breed looks like."

"He's an ally," she said, "in case you forgot that you might need them."

I hesitated, debating with myself. Suffer a demon to live? Could I do that? More, could there really come a time when I would need a demon's help?

"You haven't killed Deacon," said my sister, who was suddenly one hell of a lot older than fourteen.

I lowered the knife, grateful at least that I'd already nailed a hit of the dark that night.

"Very well, Morwain," I said, my voice haughty. I shooed my hand to the side, indicating the alleyway. "Leave us."

"Yes, mistress. Yes, yes. If you have need, you have only to call for Morwain." And then he drew a circle in the air with his hand, creating a spinning gray-black maelstrom. He aimed one last bow in my direction, then leaned into the swirling mass.

Within seconds, he was gone, the gray swirling in on itself behind him, until there was nothing but air, and Rose and I were once again alone in the alley.

"Whoa," Rose said.

I had to agree. Good to remember that I wasn't the only one in this new world of mine who could call up portals and move through them.

"Come on," I said, taking her arm and hurrying her to the pub's back door. As weird as the whole situation had been, I had to admit that the encounter with Morwain was the most pleasant demonic run-in I'd had in this particular alley. And Rose did have a point: If I was going to be a demon magnet, better to attract demons that wanted to worship me than demons that wanted to kill me.

I pulled the rust-covered door open, then ushered Rose inside. The place was deserted, of course, and we moved down the dank, stone corridor that was part of the building's original construction. The pub had been around for centuries, dating back to the old witch-hunting era. The front part of the place had been renovated about a million times since then, but the back section, with its labyrinth of stone corridors and chiseled stairs leading down to musty storage rooms and mystical ceremonial chambers, had remained mostly untouched.

And, yeah, I really did mean mystical ceremonial chambers. Alice's family had been deep into the dark arts although her mom had wanted to break free of family tradition. Alice's uncle Egan, however, had fought his sister on that little point and ended up killing her in order to keep the pub operating on the edges of the occult. He'd welcomed demonic forces, giving them a place to gather and, more important, supplying them with a stream of victims for their demonic rituals.

One of those victims, in fact, had been Alice.

Needless to say, I hadn't much liked Egan once I'd learned that little fact. And, yeah, I killed him.

About that, I had absolutely no guilt.

I'd asked Madame Parrish why me, and I think the same question held true for Alice. Yes, she had a closer connection to the demonic than I did, but still I couldn't help but wonder: Why her? Why did the demons want her dead? Why did they want to put me in this particular body?

Was it because of Deacon's vision? Because he believed that he and Alice would close the Ninth Gate together? Had the demons learned of what he'd seen, and had they been afraid?

Was there some other reason I hadn't yet thought of?

Or was it simply a matter of being born into the wrong family? A celestial case of being at the wrong place at the wrong time?

I didn't know, but I couldn't shake the feeling that the question was both important and relevant. I just wasn't sure how.

I'd never been to the upstairs apartment, but the door to the staircase was located right beside the walk-in refrigerator, and although I doubted that the pub key would work, it turned out to be a moot point, as the door wasn't locked.

The actual apartment was a different story, and as I tugged on the locked door and cursed, Rose stepped in as the voice of reason and found the key above a wall-mounted sconce.

I slid the key into the lock, turned, and the two of us stepped into the apartment.

The place was a study in contradictions, masculine, sports-related minimalism contrasting with bright colors and live flowers. And all that contrasted by exotic antiques and ancient books stacked on black-lacquered shelves. Weird, I thought, as Egan hadn't struck me as the flower type. Much less the antique type.

"Check this out," Rose said, poking inside an open box. "Old books and a bunch of magazines addressed to Rachel. And this box is filled with clothes," she said, peering into another one.

Reality clicked. Sometime within the last few days, Rachel had decided to move in. I supposed it made sense. After all, we'd inherited the place, and she was determined to make a going business of it, as opposed to the always debt-ridden establishment that Egan had run, filling in the cash gaps by selling a variety of occult items to the demons. Everything from ceremonial herbs to sacrificial virgins. Quite the entrepreneur, my late, great, uncle Egan.

My revelation made the strange decorating choices in the apartment make more sense. The bright colors weren't Egan's; they were Rachel's. At least, I assumed they were. The bright, happy colors were a stark contrast to the blacks and reds with which she'd decorated her previous home. But Rachel was no longer embracing her family's dark heritage, so I supposed this divestiture was meant to reflect her new style.

"Can I have something to eat?" Rose asked.

"Sure," I said, with absolutely no guilt. If Rachel was my sister, then she was Rose's sister, too. More or less, anyway. Besides, I couldn't even remember the last time we ate, so I knew Rose had to be starving.

She headed off to the kitchen, and I followed, then helped myself to a beer from the refrigerator. Rose settled at the small table with a bag of Chips Ahoy, a Diet Coke, and an apple, and I slid into a chair across from her, then reached for a cookie.

We ate in silence for a while, but not the comfortable kind. There were things unsaid, and they hung between us, breathing our air and making the space thick and murky and heavy. It was as if we had a silent competition going on, and whoever spoke first lost.

Rose decided to throw the game. "It's going to get bad, isn't it?"

"Yeah," I said. "I think it really is." I ran my fingers through my hair, thinking about what was happening and about what Morwain represented: an out that didn't involve pain and suffering. Demonic royalty carried its own price, sure. But one that didn't include me burning for eternity. And had the added bonus of sycophant little demons like Morwain running around doing my bidding.

But I wasn't tempted. Really, I wasn't.

At least, that was what I told myself.

"Oh, hell," I said, then scooted my chair over next to Rose. I wrapped my arm around her shoulders, and she leaned against me, her breath coming soft and easy. A domestic scene we'd repeated dozens of times before and which should have been comforting in its familiarity but was, instead, perverse. Because there wasn't really a damn thing familiar about it. Everything had changed. We weren't even the same people anymore, inside or out.

But at the core of it, she was still my sister. That was my anchor. The thing I could clutch tight to counter the dark that was always trying to claw its way to the very edges of my soul.

"Try to get some sleep," I said. "You'll feel better."

She protested some more but then disappeared into the single bedroom. I watched her enviously. Lord knew I wanted to slide into that peaceful oblivion, but I couldn't. I was too hyped. Too worried—about Deacon, about Rose, about Rachel.

And let's not forget the impending end of the world.

Deacon believed that one more key existed, and I really hoped he was right, but I had reason to doubt. For one thing, Deacon had heard only rumors. For another, we'd already tried to find the damn thing, and so far had found no hard evidence that such a key existed. Still, I had to keep looking because my other choices were vile.

In the meantime, I needed to keep the *Oris Clef* out of demonic hands. A talisman that gave the bearer power to rule over all demonkind was something that any demon worth his salt would want to get his hands on. Morwain's professed loyalty was a side bonus, but not a position I suspected the majority of the demon population would share. Still, though, a good many demons might fall in behind me, believing that it made sense to get in my good graces if I was poised to be their new ruler.

More powerful demons, however, wouldn't stand for it. So I'd have the freaks and geeks aligned with me, while the school bullies did their best to take away my lunch money.

Which meant that I could expect more and more attacks from demons with clout on earth, and also from hell-dimension dwellers like Penemue.

And wasn't that going to be fun?

For that matter, I expected that the archdemon Kokbiel would be making an appearance soon. He and Penemue had both been searching for the *Oris Clef*, but Kokbiel had been incredibly sneaky about it, using Lucas Johnson to do his dirty work. And even if Kokbiel didn't burst up through the ground like some sort of prehistoric monster, I expected that Johnson would show his ugly face. We'd saved Rose from him, but he was still out there, his demonic essence still alive in a hideous, mouthless body that would surely find and torment me soon.

I might be Lily Carlyle, Demon Assassin, but right then, I think a more accurate description would be Lily Carlyle, Demon Target with Big Red Bull's-Eye Painted on Her Ass.

And, of course, the demons weren't my only problem. Gabriel believed that I was going to become the demon queen, and he didn't seem the type to stand idly around while he waited to see what I did come convergence day. Which meant that while I was protecting my back against demons, I also needed to be covering my ass from angels.

Between all that hiding and fighting, I had to wonder when I'd have time to search for Deacon's mythical key.

Not to mention the fact that during all of that I needed to watch out for Rose. Because unless Gabriel and the demons were brain-dead, they had to know that the best way to get to me was to go through my sister.

And I already knew that Johnson was aware of that little weakness in me. He'd exploited it twice, after all.

All in all, me and mine were basically screwed, and at the moment I was fresh out of ideas about what to do next.

I was pondering the woeful state of my plan of action when the front door pushed inward, the flat surface of the door itself blocking my view. I stood, my hand going to my blade, not knowing who was on the other side. I hoped it was Rachel, but at this point, I really wasn't taking chances.

FIVE

"Oh my God!" Rachel cried, dropping the box she was carrying and sending papers shooting out across the floor in all directions. "What are you—? When did you—?"

I slid my knife back into the sheath as Rose appeared in the bedroom doorway, her face soft with sleep.

"We need to talk," I said, indicating one of the chairs at the table. Rose padded to the refrigerator and helped herself to a soda, then trotted to the table as well. I wanted to tell her to head right back into the bedroom and let me handle things, but I stopped myself. She might be a kid, but she was neck deep in this mess with me, and she had a right to at least know what was going on.

"What's going on?" Rachel asked, pulling out a chair and settling beside Rose. "Why have you guys been gone for so long? I've been calling your apartment every damn day."

"Long story," I said. "Basically, we lost about a week. And then some."

"Excuse me?"

"You first. What happened at Deacon's?"

She looked so surprised by the question that I anticipated the answer even before she articulated it: nothing.

Which was exactly what she said. Then she lifted a shoulder, looking a little sheepish as she did so. "When Deacon came back to get Rose, he told me to stay because I'd be safe there. But he didn't say for how long. And at first I was fine. I hung out on the couch and watched bad television, which I never do, and I called it a forced vacation. I mean, I needed it, you know?"

"Sure," I said. Right then, I could totally understand the allure of a lazy vacation day. "And then?"

"He said I could help myself to anything in his kitchen, and he had a nice Cabernet, so I had a few glasses. And then I must have fallen asleep on the couch, because the next thing I knew I was awake and some infomercial about a carpet-cleaning system was blaring on the television. And when I looked at the clock, I saw that it was after five in the morning. You guys had been gone for hours, and considering Lucy and Ethel were probably peeing all over my floor, I figured if I didn't get home soon, I was going to need to pay closer attention to that damn commercial."

"But he'd told you to stay," Rose said.

"I didn't think he meant forever." She spread her hands as if apologizing. "Look, I had the dogs. I had the pub. And I didn't have a clue what had happened to you or Deacon or anything."

"So where are the dogs?" Rose asked.

"I've been going over to my old place once or twice a day, and I have a neighbor looking in on them. I'll move them in here permanently when I finally get all my stuff shifted over. They don't adjust well to change, you know?"

"I'm thrilled the dogs didn't pee all over your floor," I said, "but you could have been killed."

"I wasn't," she said, then squeezed her eyes shut as she drew in three deep breaths. "But I sure thought you had been."

"No," Rose said. "We just lost time. It was really freaky."

Rachel shot Rose an odd look, then shifted her gaze to me. "Okay, what's going on? Where's Rose? And why are you acting so odd?" she added, this time addressing the question to Rose, who she clearly thought was Kiera.

I cocked my head toward Rose. "Rachel, meet my sister, Rose."

For a second, Rachel just sat there. Then she leaned back slowly, pressed her lips together, and nodded as if in time to some inner song.

"We got Johnson out of Rose," I explained. "But Kiera—"

"Kiera paid the price," Rachel whispered, holding

out her hand for Rose, who took it gratefully. "There's always a price with demons. Remember that. Nothing's free. *Nothing*."

I nodded. That much, I'd figured out all on my own.

"And Deacon?"

"That's a bit more complicated. We managed to piss off a pretty powerful demon—"

"Penemue," Rose said. "He's the one who wants—"

"The *Oris Clef*," I said. "I guess he thinks we're close to finding it."

Out of the corner of my eye, I could see Rose's brow furrow.

"Are you?" Rachel asked.

"I wish," I said, lifting my chin to fortify the lie. "Would be nice to have a bargaining chip like that."

"No kidding," Rachel said. "Dangerous, though."

"You've got that right." I lifted a shoulder in a half-hearted shrug. "Then again, this whole thing is dangerous. And getting more so."

"Deacon turned into a demon," Rose said simply, a statement that very nicely segued the conversation away from the fact that I actually had in my possession the means not only to control the demon population but to set myself up to be the supreme ruler of their universe.

It wasn't that I didn't trust Rachel . . . It was just that with her rather shady background, I figured I couldn't be too careful. After all, when you added it all up, I'd really only known her for a couple of days. I *wanted* to trust her, but I no longer trusted easily. I'd trusted Clarence, and look where that had gotten me. My supposedly heavenly handler had been working for the big bad all along.

Psych!

Not a scenario I wanted to repeat.

I thought of Deacon and frowned. Because despite having seen him turn into something as nasty as Penemue—and despite knowing that he was a demon and could be playing me—I really did trust him. Not that I'd admitted as much to him, but it was time I admitted it to myself. *I trusted Deacon.*

I did.

I thought, though, of the way he refused to let me into his head—his constant refusal to let me see the things he'd done when he was at his demonic worst. And as I thought, an unpleasant possibility occurred to me. What if Deacon had never been about redemption? After all, it had been handed to him on a platter; all he had to do was turn me over. But he hadn't. So, what if he'd ripped me away from Gabriel not because he wanted to close the gate with me and earn a place in heaven but because he didn't want me to close the gate at all?

What if, like Clarence before him, he'd been playing with my head all along?

No.

I knew better than that. At one time, Deacon had had the *Oris Clef* in his possession, and he'd tried to destroy it. Would a demon intent on ushering in the Apocalypse do that? I didn't think so.

Bottom line? I knew the man—or I wanted to think I did.

He might not have let me completely in his head yet, but for better or for worse, I trusted him.

I only hoped it was for better.

Rachel was looking at me steadily, her expression both understanding and sad, and I knew she realized that I was holding back. I met her eyes and shrugged in apology. Her head moved, the motion so minimal it couldn't even really be called a nod. But I knew we understood each other.

Rose, however, was clueless, and she was looking between the two of us, her brow furrowed. "What? What?"

She might be walking around in the body of a damn warrior chick, but inside, she was still fourteen years old.

"Your sister's being cautious," Rachel said.

"But—"

"No. It's okay." Rachel laid a soft hand on Rose's cheek. "After what the two of you have been through, she's right to be."

I could tell Rose didn't get it. Right then, though, she was the one who had to trust—in me.

"At any rate," I said, picking up the thread of conversation that we'd let unravel, "the big bad demon was pretty much trying to do us in, but Deacon pulled out a few tricks and got us out of there."

"He changed? You saw him? As a demon?"

"Yeah. He was kind of hard to miss."

"He saved our butts," Rose added helpfully. "But then he turned all scary and told us to run. And to find the key that's supposedly still out there."

"And now I'm a little worried," I admitted. "I'm afraid that he may not be able to, you know, go back."

"I bet he's okay," Rachel said. "He's not—"

"What?"

"He's not like the others."

"I know. That's why I'm worried. He's fought so hard. If he falls back now, because of me—" I ran my fingers through my hair, not even wanting to think about it. "Doesn't matter," I said briskly. "Deacon's not the problem right now. You are."

Rachel's brows lifted. "Am I?"

"Big nasty demon, remember? The one I was fighting? The one Deacon rescued me from?"

She stared at me blankly.

"I don't want him coming after you," I said. "Take a vacation, Rachel. Go visit friends in London. Go to the beach. Go shopping in New York City. Just go." I half considered having her take Rose with her, but there was no way that plan would work. I needed to be in Boston, where everything was going down. But if Rachel took Rose to London, the smart demon would snatch my little sister there, just to fuck with me.

No, Rose stayed by my side. Always.

"Go? I own half this place. There's work to do here."

"I'll handle it," I said, which was a complete lie, as the last thing I had time to do was tend bar. The real answer was, "I'll lock the place up tight until the convergence," but I didn't say that out loud. If I did, she wouldn't go. And she really had to go. Had to get safely out of Boston; and then, if the world was still a happy place in two weeks—"happy" being a relative term—she could come back, because that would mean that I'd managed to stop the hordes from crossing over.

And if the world wasn't happy?

Well, in that case, I figured Rachel would have bigger problems than a half-ownership interest in an out-of-business pub.

"Screw that," she said. "I meant what I said before. I want to help. I need to help."

"You can't," I said bluntly. At the moment, coddling was so not on my agenda. "I can't split my focus trying to protect you in a fight, Rachel."

She turned her head, pointedly looking at Rose.

"She did pretty good," I admitted reluctantly. "We had a little run-in on the way over here."

"Pretty good?" Rose said. "Watch this." She whipped out her knife, and in one fluid motion sent it flying through the air until it lodged, nice and firm, in the middle of a family portrait that hung on the wall. Specifically, I noticed, the blade had sunk deep into the space between Egan's eyes.

"Wow," I said. And, yeah, I'll admit I was impressed.

"I practiced in the bedroom before going to sleep," she said. She shot a sheepish grin toward Rachel. "I didn't want Lily to hear, so, um, your pillow's a little mangled."

I bit back a grin. Once upon a time, Rose had been a spunky kid, but Johnson had stolen that from her. She was getting it back, though, and as perverse as it sounded, being in Kiera's body was actually helping. She wasn't the same girl in the same body attracting the same demon anymore.

She was in the body of a fighter. A girl with pink hair, an attitude, and the trained body of a kick-ass warrior. Honestly, I wasn't sure I wanted my sister to be a warrior, though. At the same time, I didn't think I had a choice.

Rachel pointed toward the knife. "Okay, I admit it. No way can I do that."

"Which is why I want you to get out of here."

"*But*," she said, holding up a hand to shut me up, "I can still be useful. And the kind of useful that you're going to want around."

Maybe I should have told her to forget it, but I didn't. Because I did need help. And, yeah, I was curious. "All right. I'm listening."

"You need to be strong, right? I mean, really strong?"

I shoved my hands into my pockets. "Yeah. Considering what I'm up against, yeah."

"Well, then," she said. "I can help. You told me how you get stronger. I can help you do that. We talked about this, remember? And I still really want to help."

"How I get stronger?" I repeated. "I get stronger by

killing demons." An act which had the rather unpleasant downside of also making me more demonic. Darker. Hungry for a fight, for the pain. And, like a drug, whenever I thought about it, the craving to kill and become just a little bit more like my prey snuck up on me. Slowly at first, and then overwhelming. Sucking me in and drawing me under.

I didn't want it. And yet . . .

And yet, I did.

I closed my eyes and forced myself to gather. I didn't need help finding demons to kill. The last thing I needed was to feed that habit.

"You've gotta, Lily," Rose said, her voice almost a whisper. "You've gotta get as strong as you can." She pulled her knees up to her chest and hugged them. "This is big stuff. I mean, you saw Deacon. You saw Penemue. And the way Johnson got inside me even though I didn't want him there and tried so hard to push him out of me."

"Rose . . ." My voice hitched in my throat, but she didn't stop. She'd started to say her piece, and she wasn't pausing until she'd had her chance.

"You're supposed to be some super demon fighter, but I saw it on your face, and you're scared." It wasn't an accusation, merely a statement of fact.

For a moment, I considered denial, but I couldn't do it. I owed my sister the truth.

"Yeah," I admitted. "I'm scared. But I'm not going to hide." And, yeah, I was going to do whatever was necessary to get me ready for the Big Leagues. And if that meant I killed demons—if that meant I let the dark build up inside me like a sweet, viscous oil—then that was what I was going to do. But I had enough to worry about with Rose. Adding Rachel to the mix was simply too many people to watch out for.

"You're not the only one who can find the demons," I said. "Kiera could smell them."

I nodded toward Rose, whose eyes were wide. "Yeah? Well, maybe she could, but I can't. I told you so on the street."

"Are you certain?"

"I had some demon jerk's slimy tentacle around my waist and another one pulling me up by my shirt, and didn't smell a thing. And with the Three Stooges on the street, all I caught a whiff of was their nasty sweat. Trust me," she said, tapping her nose. "This isn't a demon sniffer."

"I can pick them out," Rachel said. "Benefit of being a Purdue." Her mouth twitched. "Guess you need me after all. Sis," she added, with a big, wide smile.

I made a face but conceded the point. The truth was, unless they had fangs, slime, or cloven feet, I had no skill for picking a demon out of a crowd.

I sighed, resigned. "Fine. You stay. You help."

She leaned back in her chair, her expression smug. "Excellent."

"But you shut down the kitchen. The demons come in, it's for drinks only. And you serve them," I said, pointing a stern finger. "Send Gracie and Trish and everybody on a vacation," I said, referring to the waitresses. I stifled a sigh at the thought of Gracie. She'd been one of Alice's closest friends, and I genuinely liked her. More than that, I missed her. I hated that she was so in the dark, but I'd hate it more if she got hurt. "Better yet, actually buy them the plane tickets. Let's get them out of town. Caleb, too," I said, referring to the cook.

Rachel tilted her head to the side and examined me, and I braced myself for the mother of all arguments. To my surprise, she merely nodded. "Okay," she said. "No civilians near the pub. And I'll see about the vacation. Maybe a cabin at a lake somewhere."

I'll admit I was impressed that Rachel was getting with the program. But still I scowled. "I don't like it. It's dangerous. And you're just . . . Well, you're just you." I made a face. "No offense."

She laughed. "None taken."

"I just mean that it's dangerous. This pub is a demon magnet. Do you really want to stay here?"

"One, I really want to help. And two, I'm safe in the pub."

"That's bullshit," I said. "For that matter, I think you're insane to move in here. You should—"

"Would you trust me?" she interrupted. "The place has been protected for centuries."

I cocked my head. "Protected? What do you mean?"

"Exactly what I said. When my family first offered the pub up as a demon gathering ground, a deal was struck. No harm can come to us from the demons inside the building."

"Well, that's bullshit," I said. "In case you forgot, Alice was killed by demons."

"Not here," Rachel said.

I wasn't sure if that was true or not, but I suspected it was. I tried another tack. "What about those two thug-oid demons that attacked me a while back right by the bar? Inside the pub. With no mystical, magical protection working overtime to keep me safe."

"But you're not really part of the family, are you?"

She had a point.

"And how about Egan? I killed him."

She laughed. "I didn't say we couldn't be harmed here. Just not harmed by demons."

"Oh," I said, a little surge of relief slipping into my soul. At least as of the morning I killed Egan, I was still more human than demon. That, I thought, was something.

"And you can really spot the demons?"

"I already told you so."

"How?"

"Most of them I know. You work here long enough, and you pick things up. But they do have a distinctive scent. Everyone in my family's pretty attuned to it."

"What about outside the pub?" I asked. "Can they harm you there?"

She held me fast in her steady gaze. "The world's not a safe place, Lily, no matter how much you might wish it were."

Okay. She had a point.

"You don't have to do this," I said.

"They killed my sister," she countered. "I do."

And with that, I really couldn't argue.

"So," she said, her voice rising along with her body as she pushed up out of her chair, returning with a felt-tip pen and one of the pads of paper that had tumbled from her box. "What's your game plan?" she asked, as she printed "STOP APOCALYPSE" in block letters at the top of the pad.

"My best bet is to find this key that Deacon says is rumored to exist."

"Find the rumored key," Rachel scrawled. "So how do we do that?"

Rose peered at the pad, then leaned back with a snort.

Rachel shot her a sharp look.

"Sorry," my sister said, tossing up her hands. "I guess I just figured I was done with school, what with being in a new body and the impending Apocalypse and all." Her lips twitched. "Is there going to be a pop quiz?"

"You may be stronger than me," Rachel said, pointing her pen with menace, "but I'm still older than you, and I will give you a spanking. Or I'll try," she admitted, which took a little fire out of the whole discipline routine.

"Shut up, Rose. Frankly, we need a plan." At the moment, my plan went something like, *Kill demons; prevent end of world.* If Rachel could add order and direction, I was all for that.

"Like I said, how do we go about finding this key?" Rachel asked.

Rose lifted one shoulder in an exasperated shrug. "Well, that's the whole point, right? We don't have a clue."

"What about another demon?" Rachel said. "Maybe we should catch one and ask it. Or, you know, ask it really persuasively. Like bamboo-under-the-toenails persuasive." She frowned. "Then again, a demon might actually like that."

"It's a good idea," I admitted. "And if I have the chance to capture and interrogate a demon, I'll do just that. But in the meantime, I have a better idea. Father Carlton."

"Who?" Rachel asked.

"The priest," I said, my stomach twisting with the memory. "The priest the demons tricked me into killing."

"But if he's dead . . . ?" Rose asked.

"He must have staff," Rachel said, excited. "An assistant. A what-do-you-call-it? An altar boy, or a deacon or something."

"But how do we find them?" Rose asked. "Just call churches and ask if they have a dead priest named Father Carlton? What if he wasn't even from Boston?" She turned to me. "Clarence told you the portal opened here, right? So Father Carlton could have flown here from Kansas for all we know."

"She has a point," Rachel said, frowning.

"Deacon," I said.

Rachel frowned. "Yeah, but we can't talk to the altar boys or the deacons or anybody who might have helped him until we know where he came from."

"No, I mean the man. Deacon. Deacon Camphire." I looked between Rose and Rachel. "I need to find him. He knew about Father Carlton and what he was doing. So he probably also knows what church Father Carlton came from." That wasn't the only reason I wanted to find Deacon, of course, but it was a biggie.

Rachel poised the pen on her paper, then hesitated. "If you find him, and he's still in his demon state . . ."

I nodded. "Yeah," I said. "But I need to find him anyway. We tried, but we didn't have any luck. What about you? You were in his house. Can you find your way back?"

"I don't remember leaving," she said, as calmly as if she were commenting on the weather.

"And that's relevant because . . . ?"

"Protections," Rachel said. "Spells. Deacon's done something to his house, so that you don't remember anything about it once you leave."

"That's completely fucked-up," I said. "I'll never find him."

"Your arm?"

"Only works for objects," Rose said. "I already tried that suggestion."

"But not a problem," Rachel said. "Because, see? We have our plan, and all we have to do is slide Deacon into the proper place." She did just that, writing "Find Father Carlton's peeps." Then, under that, she added "DEACON-R" and "BOSTON CHURCHES-R" in perfect block lettering.

"R?" I asked.

"Me," she said, snapping the cap back on the pen.

I shook my head, confused. "You're going to call the churches and ask about Father Carlton—I get that. But you don't know where Deacon's house was. So how do you think you're going to find him?"

"Easy," she said, with a Cheshire cat kind of grin. "Follow me down to the bar, and I'll show you."

SIX

"And you're going to do what?" I asked, as Rachel led us through the kitchen and into the pub.

"Patience," Rachel said, sliding easily behind the U-shaped oak-hewn bar, but not giving me a clue as to what she was planning. I tapped my foot, growing more and more frustrated. After all, *I* was the kick-ass demon killer. Yet I was the one standing around with my thumb up my ass not having any idea what was going on. What was wrong with *that* picture?

She motioned for us to take our seats, then sighed, exasperated, when we were interrupted by a sharp tapping on the front window.

"Hang on," she said, then went to the door. I followed her, wary. Yes, I remembered what she said about not being vulnerable while she was inside the pub, but as far as I was concerned, that particular enchantment remained unproven.

"Jarel," she said, peering through the glass. She flipped the locks and opened the door. "We're not open right now."

A scraggly red-haired man in a silver-studded biker jacket and filthy black jeans stepped closer. "Since when you stop opening at ten, Rachel?"

"Sorry, Jarel," she said. "We're short-staffed."

He leaned forward, peering at me, then into the bar and at Rose. "Looks like you got enough folks in here to serve me a pint."

"Closed," Rachel said firmly, then started to push the door. His foot went into the space, blocking the door from closing all the way. I stepped forward, wondering if I was going to need to intervene between Rachel and the obnoxious customer.

But Rachel had it under control. "Give it up, Jarel. We're closed. But if you come back at five, the Guinness is on the house."

"Yeah?"

"Absolutely."

"That's something."

He retreated, and she locked up, then pulled the velvet curtains over the windows to block any further interruptions.

"Loyal clientele," I said.

"Demon," she said. "Pretty nasty one, too. But he always pays his bills on time."

I glanced back at the door and sighed. Unless he'd come at me with a knife, I wouldn't have picked him out of a lineup as a demon. Apparently Rachel really did know what she was doing. About spotting demons, anyway. About this Deacon-finding thing, I was still dubious.

"He's one of the ones I was going to point out to you later today," she added.

"What?"

"To kill," she said easily. "To make you stronger." She glanced back toward the door. "He's the kind who'd rip your head off if he thought you had a chance of closing the gate. Kill him. Get stronger. And make the world a better place."

"Maybe," I said, temptation welling within me. On the one hand, the mere thought of a demon kill got me all jazzed up. On the other hand, did I really need to be running around risking my hide for a hit? Even if I might be making the demon-ridden streets that much safer.

"Just saying," Rachel said.

"Let's just focus on Deacon," I said as I once again took my seat. "What exactly are you going to do?"

"Scry," she said, and I nodded sagely because I didn't want to admit that I had no idea what she was talking about.

Rose, thank goodness, wasn't so prideful. "Huh?"

"Scrying is a way of seeing things psychically. It's not a common ability, but it is one of my gifts. All the women in my family have been able to scry." She looked at me. "Except for Alice. Her visions took a different form."

I nodded wryly. At first, I'd assumed the sight was

part of my new Prophecy Girl persona, but I learned soon enough that not only had it come from Alice but my demonic handlers had no knowledge that I had the gift. And even before I'd realized they'd duped me, I'd kept the sight secret. What can I say? I'd always been a bit of a rebel, and even though I thought I was working for heaven, I couldn't just leave my old personality on the doorstep, could I?

At any rate, it was because of Alice's sight that I'd been able to peek into Rachel's head, and I trusted her (more or less) despite her past ventures into the dark arts. And it was because of the sight that I knew that Deacon—though once confined to the darkest pits of hell—craved redemption with a passion intense enough to consume both of us.

And it was because of the sight that I'd been able to see the future through Gabriel's eyes—a future in which all of the demons in the world bowed down before me.

A future that could come to pass, I knew. But one that I told myself I didn't want, despite the dark bits inside me rising to challenge that assessment. Or, rather, *because* of those dark bits.

I shivered and prayed for both strength and the lost key. Because if I could get that damn gate closed and locked with Deacon's supposedly missing key, then the temptation to use the *Oris Clef* would vanish.

At least, I hoped it would.

"So what do you do?" Rose asked.

"You've seen it done in movies and things, I'm sure," Rachel said. "Crystal gazing."

"Yeah?" Rose leaned in to peer over the bar into the work area where Rachel now stood. "You have a crystal ball back there?"

Rachel shook her head. "I take a slightly different approach."

As we watched, she pulled down five different brands of vodka, followed by three different brands of gin. She put the bottles on the bar in two rows, then turned her attention to me. "Run and dim the lights, would you?"

I did, then returned through the velvety black, which was broken only by the single brass lamp that sat behind the bar, its low-wattage light casting a dim orange glow.

"Perfect," Rachel said.

"So you can find Deacon?" Rose asked. "How about the key? Can you find that, too?" She shifted in her seat to face me. "I mean, if he's all ookey-demoney, then maybe we should skip Deacon altogether and just shoot for the big prize."

A damn good plan, actually. Too bad Rachel shot it down. "Only people." She lifted a shoulder. "Well, only living energy, which means humans and demons who have taken on a living form within this dimension."

"Oh." I clasped my hands together and tried not to think about the thought that was pounding inside my head: If Deacon had gone over into some other dimension, then this all might end without my ever seeing him again.

From somewhere behind the bar, Rachel pulled out a small black candle. She placed it in front of the collection of bottles, lit it, then turned behind her to switch off the brass lamp. The single flame danced in the dark, the light reflecting on the glass bottles and the clear liquid within. Rachel closed her eyes, then drew her hand over the flame, so close I knew that her palm must be burning, but no pain reflected on her face. Instead, she tilted her head back, then leaned forward and opened her eyes.

When she did, they appeared to burn, as if the flame she had touched had traveled through her to her eyes. She spread her hands so that her fingers seemed to call to the bottles, and her entire being was focused solely on the liquid within.

Rose and I might as well have not existed, and I reached blindly for Rose's hand, then squeezed tight, wondering if I should stop the ritual. I was afraid Rachel was sliding back into the dark arts from which she had broken away. And if she did that, I feared that she, like Deacon, would get sucked back into her past.

I leaned forward, prepared to reach out and shake her and try to break the trance, but I couldn't do it. I wanted too desperately to see Deacon. And as much as I hated myself for letting Rachel put her toe back into the dark to satisfy my own needs, I wasn't willing to make her stop. Not when I knew that I stood on the precipice of sacrificing so much more of myself than a toe.

I squeezed Rose's hand, hating myself, and wondering how a person as selfish as me could be expected to save the whole goddamned world.

"He is alone," Rachel said, in a voice not her own. "He is alone. And he is waiting."

"What for?" I whispered, not even certain she could hear me.

Apparently, she could. Her head turned slowly toward me, as the rest of her body stayed utterly still. "For you," she said. And then her eyes rolled back in her head, and she fell to the floor.

"Holy crap!" Rose called.

I silently seconded that assessment, even as I vaulted over the bar, almost knocking down her little arrangement of vodka and gin bottles as I did. "Rachel!" I scooped my arms under her shoulders and forced her upright. "Rachel, dammit, answer me."

Her body shook as if she were coming off a really bad high, her teeth chattering as I hugged her close, trying to get her warm. "Blanket," I said to Rose, who was halfway across the pub before the word was even out of my mouth.

"Rach! Rachel! Are you okay? Dammit, you shouldn't have done that!"

"F-fine," she said. "W-will be f-fine."

"It's black magic," I hissed, "and you gave that shit up. I should never have let you—"

Her hand closed tight around my wrist. "My choice," she said, and this time, her voice and her eyes were clear. "My choice." She drew in a noisy breath, her lungs rattling as if they were filled with gunk. "And it's only black if you use it for black." She reached up to cup my face. "I was using it for you. I was using it for good."

Her eyes closed, and her shoulders slumped again in exhaustion.

I held her close, hoping like hell that she was right.

SEVEN

"Where is he? Where is he?" Rose called, as she raced back with a blanket. "Did she find him? Does she know where he is?"

"Bridge," Rachel said, her voice soft and breathy.

"Quiet," I said, pressing a damp bar towel to her forehead. "Just sit for a minute."

"Holy crap," Rose said, skidding to a stop near the bar. "Holy crap, holy crap. Is she okay?"

"I think so," I said.

"I'm fine," Rachel said, struggling to get up.

I held her down. "Forget it. You're going to sit right here on the floor and drink a brandy. You look like shit."

"Thanks a lot." She pressed her fingers to her temple and winced. "But I will take a brandy."

I nodded to Rose to pour one, which was a mistake

because she proceeded to stare at the bottles, her mouth slightly open as she perused each of the labels.

"There," Rachel finally said, pointing helpfully toward the far side of the bar.

"Oh. Right." A few moments later, Rose handed Rachel the glass. And not long after that I rocked back on my heels, examined her face, and pronounced the woman healthy enough to tell us what the fuck had just happened.

"It drains me," she said, then shrugged as if she were embarrassed. "It never drained my mother. She used to gaze into the dishwater every morning. Some days it would show her what would happen to us that day. Some days she'd see years into the future." She pointed at me. "She never told us, but I think she knew that Alice was going to die."

"Really? Why?"

"Nothing specific. Just a feeling I had. She used to treat Alice like she wasn't entirely permanent." She shook her head, as if she was trying to sort her thoughts. "Probably my imagination. But I do know for sure that she saw something mysterious about Alice at least once."

"How do you know that?" I'd been living in Alice for a while, but she'd died before I moved in, so I still didn't feel like I knew the girl. Everything I'd learned had been through her friends, her mail, or her medicine cabinet.

"Mom's the reason Alice got that," Rachel said, pointing her finger at my left breast.

"Excuse me?"

"Not the boob," Rachel said. "The tattoo."

"Really?" Alice had a tiny dagger tattoo on her breast that I'd wondered about since day one. "Why? What did she see?"

"No idea," Rachel said. "But Alice would have been about thirteen. Mom and I were doing dishes, and she saw something. And Mom left the dishes in the sink and stormed up to Alice's bedroom and took her to a tattoo parlor right then."

"Wow," Rose said.

"Yeah, no kidding," Rachel agreed. "I didn't even like tattoos, but I remember begging to get one, too. I guess I thought it was cool or something, but Mom said no."

"Did Alice ever tell you what your mom saw?"

"I don't think Mom even told Alice," Rachel said.

"And she saw whatever it was in the dishwater?" Rose said, her lip curling. "You have *so* got to be kidding me."

Rachel laughed, then reached for Rose's hand. "I promise you, I'm not. Mother could scry with any shiny surface, though. I think she just liked to show off with the bubbles."

"And you?"

"Bottles only." She exhaled, then climbed to her feet, and I got the distinct feeling that the discussion about Alice's breasts was over. My curiosity, however, had been mightily piqued.

I turned my attention back to Rachel, ready to

steady her if she toppled over. "I'm okay," she said, then slid out from behind the bar and moved to a nearby table. "But it does take a lot out of me."

"So back to Rose's original question," I said. "Where is he?"

"The bridge," Rachel said dully. "The Zakim Bridge." She turned her face toward me. "But don't go, Lily. He's not . . . He's not himself."

Her words twisted in my heart. He'd taken back his demonic form so that he could save me. But that wasn't who he was anymore, and it sure as hell wasn't who he wanted to be. And if there was even the slightest chance that his nature hadn't consumed him, I had to go to him. I had to tell him what I was going to do.

And, yeah, I had to offer him the chance to help me. And to help himself.

"He'll hurt you," Rose said. "You saw the way he looked at us."

I had, but I also saw the fight within him. "He needs me," I said, simply. I didn't completely understand it, and for a while I'd even tried to fight it, but Deacon and I were bound. Our destinies as entwined as our bodies had been. He was in my heart, and if there was even the slightest chance to save him, I knew that I had to try.

"There's not even a guarantee he's still there," Rachel said. "I didn't find him at home—I didn't even see where home is. And I doubt he's going to hang around on a bridge forever."

"That's why I need to go now," I said. "You'll stay with Rose?"

"Hello? I should go with you." She drew her blade. "You need someone to watch your back."

"I've got my own back," I said. "And I want Rachel watching yours."

"You said I stayed with you!"

"I did," I admitted. "But that was before Rachel told me about the protections on the pub."

"But I'm not family."

"They'd have to go through me to get to you," Rachel said. "And they can't do that."

"Screw this," Rose said sulkily.

"You're staying," I said, but with not quite as much force. I was afraid. Afraid of making the wrong decision and losing her.

Rachel reached out and squeezed my hand. "It's okay," she said. "We'll go into the apartment. I can add protections there."

"Rachel—"

Her smile flickered. "For good," she said. "Not for black. I'll be fine."

"I—"

"Go. You may not have much time."

"It's no fair," Rose said.

"Please," I said, moving to stand in front of my sister. "I can't deal if you argue. Just do this, okay? Stay. Stay and help Rachel find the priest."

"Fine," she said, managing to make the one word sound much more like "fuck you."

"Call me before you come back," Rachel said. "I'll see if I can find out where Jarel holes up."

"Jarel?" I tried to shift my thoughts away from Rose and come up with a face to go with the name, but nothing popped.

"The redhead," she reminded me. "The one you should—" She ended her sentence with a pantomimed knife slice across her throat.

"Oh. Right. But I'm not sure I should be risking my neck going after them. I mean, he might leave me alone."

She shrugged. "Or you might be giving him the time to gather a miniature army to take you out good and proper. Trust me when I say that I wouldn't put something like that past a guy like Jarel."

Okay, she had a point. "I'll call," I said.

"Good. In the meantime, Rose and I will dig in, right, Rose?"

"Whatever."

I bit back a laugh, because no matter how freaky our lives had become, that tone in her voice would forever mean home. And normalcy.

"My bike's at my apartment," I said to Rachel. "Can I take your car?"

She frowned, and I could practically see her saying a mental good-bye to her pristine Mercedes. "Good of mankind," I prodded. "Saving the world. All that stuff."

"Driving to meet a ferocious demon who almost killed you . . ."

"He didn't almost kill us," I said. "He just lunged at us in a really mean way."

She cast her eyes up toward heaven. At least that

was what I thought until she spoke. "Upstairs. Keys are on the hook next to the refrigerator. It's parked in the back."

"I thought you guys were going to hole up in the apartment with protections?"

She nodded toward the bar and the collection of bottles. "As soon as I put the place back together."

I left Rose sulking with Rachel, snagged the keys, then checked myself in the mirror by the apartment door. I still wasn't used to Alice's face staring back at me—I'd always been plain, not pretty, and seeing those bright green eyes and that flawless skin always threw me for a bit of a loop. The body was more functional, too. More athletic and less burdened by the baggage left over from too many Kit Kat bars.

I tugged down the collar of the tank I wore to display the dagger tattoo on my breast. Why on earth would a woman suddenly decide to tattoo her adolescent daughter? I'd marked Rose because I hadn't wanted her to forget who she was. Had Alice's mother had the same sort of motivation? Or was I seeing connections where none existed?

I didn't know, but at the moment I was hardly inclined to think about it. I adjusted my thigh holster, shrugged into my red duster, then strapped the demon's scabbard onto my back and slid his sword inside. My blade, a sword, and a switchblade. Probably not enough, but unless I was going to carry a knife block and a set of steak knives, it was all I had at the moment.

"Here goes nothing," I said to my reflection. I

looked like what I was—a warrior. And while I normally wouldn't go out on the streets of Boston looking like that, with only four days left in my countdown, I wasn't much worried about appearances.

I had a goal, and the sooner I got to the bridge, the better. I swept out of the apartment, down the stairs, and out the back door of the pub—at which point I ran smack into Jarel.

Apparently Rachel was right. He was one demon who needed killing.

"I hear you got something special hanging from round that pretty little neck of yours," Jarel said, and I winced, forcing myself to keep my hand at my side and not raise it protectively to my throat. "Don't seem fair a little thing like you would have such a fancy necklace. Does it, fellas?"

A low murmur of negatives filled the alley, and though I could see no one else, I knew they were there. Demons, hiding in the darkness. Demons, waiting to whale on my ass.

"Just try and take it," I said, with more bravado than I felt. I might be immortal, but that didn't mean I was impervious. Lots of nasty things could happen to me. Like, for example, they could cut off my legs. My arms. My head.

I could hardly find the missing key without my various appendages. And if I wasn't mobile, I wouldn't be much good at getting to the portal to toss myself in, either.

Not that I knew exactly where the portal was opening. I frowned and added that to my mental to-do list. Honestly, it was amazing how much preparation had to be made before the end of the world.

At the moment, though, I needed to be focused on staying whole and keeping the *Oris Clef* away from my buddy Jarel there. A task that, at the moment, seemed easier said than done.

They were coming at me from both ends of the alley, six on each side, and they were moving close together, as if they were one body with one purpose.

Great. A coordinated force of well-trained demons. Just what I needed.

I kept my blade sheathed and pulled out my sword. I hadn't yet made it my own, and I took care of that little detail by sliding my hand down the razor-sharp edge. A line of blood rose, and as I stared at the demons, I smeared it on my blade. "This will end you now," I said to each of them. "Make no mistake."

Unfortunately, they didn't run screaming from my announcement. So much for my scary bad-ass persona.

Just the opposite, in fact. Because two of them stepped away from one demon chorus line and started walking toward me. Then two from the other line joined the party.

Four against one, with eight held in reserve. *Not* good odds.

"Well, *hell*," I said, then went postal on their asses, swinging the sword and managing to lop off two heads with one blow. I felt like the brave little tailor, except that two demons stepped in to replace their fallen buddies, and these dudes had even bigger nasty swords. And unlike the movies, they weren't coming at me one at a time. They were all coming at once, and I *really* didn't have time for this. I needed to be out searching for Deacon. Not fighting demons. And certainly not getting my various body parts amputated.

I swung around hard and fast, slicing the gut of one of the approaching demons open. My blade was still in his belly when one of his buddies came at me from behind. I slammed my leg back, managing to nail him in the groin and send him tumbling backward into two of his buddies.

What I didn't anticipate, but should have, was the demon that lunged in from the side and grabbed my leg even as I was pulling back in from my thrust. *Jarel*, and Rachel was right—he was a mean one.

He had a solid hold on my ankle, and he twisted, forcing me to turn or lose the leg. I lunged forward as he pulled me over, leading with the sword, but my aim was seriously compromised by the fact that he was jerking me all over creation, and I ended up tumbling to the ground, landing flat on my back, the sword still in one hand but my pride utterly lost.

Not that I had time to think about pride or swords or battle plans, because Jarel was on me, his own knife out, and he was coming at me. I lashed up with the sword, hoping to slice him in two at the gut, then cried out in pain as my blade hit something metallic and solid.

Chain mail. The little fuck is actually wearing medieval-style armor under his Boston Celtics T-shirt.

Honestly, I had to admire his preparation if not his sentiment, but not too much, because he'd pretty much fucked my arm up bad. So much so that when I tried to redirect my aim to his neck, I smashed uselessly against his upper torso. My whole arm was tingling, as if it were one giant funny bone, and even though I'm much better fighting with my right hand, I transferred the sword—or I tried to. Because he dove on me midtransfer, wresting the blade from my hand and pressing the tip against my neck.

"Killed by your own blade, bitch," he said. "There isn't much less honorable than that."

"Screw you," I said, trying to figure out how the hell I would get out of this predicament.

"I should keep you alive," he said, apparently not realizing that I already had that base covered. "I'd like to see you kneel before me when I ascend to the throne. Kneel before me now," he added with a leer, "and maybe I will spare your life."

"Happy to," I said. "So long as you don't mind losing your cock when I bite down hard." I shifted, grimacing, and felt the tip of the sword cut into my flesh. *Damn.*

I really didn't have a lot of options. I was pretty much down to hoping he wouldn't actually disconnect my head, when his muscles tensed, and he whispered, "Die now." But before he had the chance to make that command a reality, he went flying sideways across the alleyway, something small and lithe clinging to him like a monkey.

I didn't bother to question the odd nature of such timely assistance. Instead, I scrabbled to my feet, grabbed my sword, which he'd dropped, and lashed out hard, mowing down two demons who were staring dumbstruck at the spectacle.

So was I, now that I turned in that direction: Morwain had latched onto Jarel, his sharp incisors yanking the skin of the demon's shoulders off, his clawed hands ripping the flesh all the way down to the bone.

I looked away. Help was one thing, but . . .

The cluster of demons did not rush to assist Jarel, but neither did they run away. Just the opposite. Morwain's attack seemed to have mobilized them, and instead of a fight, I found myself in the middle of a mob. There was no rhyme or reason, simply slashing and stabbing, thrusting and defending.

Over the din, I heard Morwain calling for support, then a second voice.

Rose.

"Get inside," I shouted, thrusting with my blade, then pulling it back out. The demon fell away in a puddle of goo, and I drew in the strength and played off it, using the demon's own essence to take down the two buddies nearest it.

Yes. Oh, heaven help me, but yes, yes, yes.

I wanted more, and I had demons for the choosing.

As the power rushed through me, I wasn't seeing the cluster of demons so much as a scary mob, but instead as a delicious buffet. And I was determined to sample it all.

"Lily! Behind you!"

I whipped around, lopping off the head of an attacking demon. "Dammit, Rose, get back inside!"

"I just saved you!"

"I would have been fine," I countered, and was rewarded with a dubious snort.

"Mistress," Morwain called. "The odds. Go. Go and protect the crown."

Honestly, I was half-tempted. If I could get inside the damn pub, maybe I could get out the front door and leave the alley to these crazed demons. I mean, I was all for reducing the demon population, but I needed to go find Deacon.

"Come on," I said to Rose. "We're going in."

Except the door burst open, and Rachel came out.

"Dammit," I cried, thrusting sideways to nail an approaching demon. "What part of 'stay safe inside' do you people not understand?"

Of course Rachel ignored me, shouting out that I needed to toss her the car keys. I didn't argue. What was the point?

As I tackled a handful of demons, Rose whacked away at another cluster, clearing Rachel's path to the car. I got a little distracted by the demon aiming at my face with a mace, but when he suddenly became roadkill—courtesy of Rachel's raging Mercedes—I had to admit that she'd caught my attention.

The demons' attention, too. There were only a handful left, and they finally scattered, bowled over not by the awe and fear they felt toward Prophecy Girl but persuaded instead by the silent purr of German engineering.

I stood in the carnage, letting the dark essence rage through me.

I tilted my head back and drew in a deep breath—and saw someone dressed all in white standing on the roof of one of the restaurants across the alley. I squinted, trying to figure out who it was.

Gabriel?

Except it didn't look a damn thing like Gabriel. And if it *was* Gabriel, why wasn't he swooping down to catch me?

Footsteps echoed behind me, and I turned to find Rachel trotting toward me. "Do you know him?" I asked, jerking my chin toward the rooftop.

She squinted, then shook her head. "Not a regular in the bar. Are you worried?"

"Not sure," I admitted. "Maybe I need to pop up there and see what he wants."

"And maybe you need to go find Deacon," Rose said. She was looking at the roof, too, her brow creased as she frowned.

"Rose? What's up?"

"Nothing," she said, although I didn't believe her.

"Do you know who that is?"

She turned to me, shoulders dropping and head tilting to one side as exasperation oozed off her. "Like I know a lot of demons?"

"You've encountered a few," I said, but her point had been made.

"I'm just saying he could be a human for all we know. Some dude who heard the fight and came to watch. But you know you have to go see Deacon, so *do* that already."

"She's right," Rachel said.

"I know she is," I said, even though I was still convinced that my little sister was playing coy. "Fine. I'm going." I pointed at Rachel. "But I want you two inside. Now. And keep the pub closed today, okay?"

Rachel crossed her arms over her chest. "I'll keep it closed today, but I'm not keeping it closed forever. For one thing, I was right about Jarel, and I can help you keep an eye out for others like him, and I can do that better if the bar's open—even if just for drinks—and they're coming inside."

"Rachel—"

She held up a hand to stop me. "For another, if the world doesn't come to an end—and it won't—this pub is our livelihood, and I am not going to shut it completely down for four full days. You understand me?"

"Just today," I said. I glanced back at the opposite rooftop, an unreasonable knot of dread twisting in my gut. "Put protections around the apartment and stay safe. Just do that for me, okay?"

She took Rose's hand, then nodded. "We'll clean.

Egan's apartment was utter filth, and I've barely made a dent."

"Great," I said, not caring what they did so long as they were inside and safe. "Awesome. Terrific."

"Go," Rose said.

And so I went.

EIGHT

The Zakim Bridge is a Boston landmark, partly because it's such a cool bridge and partly because it was part of the whole Big Dig construction project, which made its own headlines because the project was both massive and expensive.

The bridge itself is part of I-93 and runs over the Charles River, none of which is particularly interesting, but what is cool about it is the way it looks. It's a cable-stayed bridge, which probably means nothing to you unless you're an architect, but if you're looking at it from a distance, the bridge looks like it has two pyramids atop it. Not solid pyramids, but pyramids made of tons and tons of taut metal cable which rise up and attach to eighty-foot concrete towers that jut perpendicularly out of the bridge itself.

It's cool enough that photos of the bridge make up a

large percentage of Boston postcards, and, frankly, I think it gives the skyline some much-needed pizzazz.

At any rate, it's big. And although Deacon's dragony demon form was also big, I'll confess that I was hoping to meet up with his much more manageably sized human form. How I was supposed to find one man on an entire bridge, though . . . Well, I really didn't know. Especially since pedestrians are technically not allowed on the bridge. And, honestly, I felt rather grumpy about the whole thing.

Still, I needed to do this, and so I decided to take the boring, methodical approach and walk the damn thing. And, yes, I realized that was not allowed. But I was über-girl-fighter-chick, and I was in a pissy mood.

Besides, I was wearing a knife and a sword. How much more bad-ass could a girl get?

Not that it's easy to walk the bridge. For one thing, it's raised, which means that unless you want to go all Spider-Man, you have to walk a long way, starting way back from where the freeway is actually on the ground. Do that, though, and the Massachusetts Transit Authority or the Boston police or whoever the heck is in charge will toss you in the back of a black-and-white without even giving you time to blink.

Again, I had the knife, not to mention my surly inner demons, but even so, I wasn't keen on stumbling through the whole Most Wanted routine. Still, I had to find Deacon, so I started out driving, then flipped on the hazard lights about the time I was midway over the Charles River. I lifted my foot from the accelerator, let the car roll to a stop, then killed the engine. And just to make it look good, I slammed my hand down hard on the steering wheel as if I was yet one more pissed-off commuter.

When you break down on the bridge, you're supposed to pull over to the side and wait patiently for help. You're not supposed to get out of the car and start walking.

What can I say? The demons made me do it.

Since this was Boston and it wasn't 3:00 A.M., the traffic was terrible. The infamous late-lunch, early-evening drive-time rush hour. Which meant that I was risking my body (if not my life, what with being immortal and all) by walking on the little strip of asphalt that formed the shoulder. A shoulder that, honestly, did not provide room for a car to stall out. And that, frankly, was a bonus. Because I could hear the screech of brakes and the curse of commuters as they approached my supposedly stalled vehicle, then had to ease one lane over to get around it.

One particularly pissed-off soul rolled down his window, tapped his horn to get my attention, then lifted a fist to me. "Hey, lady!" he roared. "Mooove the fahkin' caaah!"

Man, do I love Boston.

I kept walking, fighting the grin that would surely piss these drivers off more. It probably was the deep, dark demons inside me, but something about mucking up the general flow of traffic gave me a nice little buzz in my belly.

I hadn't seen Deacon when I was driving, and I still didn't see him once I was walking. My general state of mind was alternating between worried and frustrated. With a large smattering of scared thrown in. Scared of what he'd become. Scared that he couldn't come back.

"Hey!" A guy in a battered green Toyota slowed beside me. "Psycho bitch! Get yo' fat ass off the road."

Okay, now, that just ticked me off. For one thing, I no longer had a fat ass. And for another thing, however accurate the psycho-bitch label might be, that was just plain rude.

I didn't pull the sword, but I did push my coat back and rest my hand on the hilt of my knife. "You want to get out of the car and say that to my face?"

Apparently he didn't, as he simply shot me the finger and hit the accelerator. *Asshole.*

I shoved my hands in my pockets, primarily because what I really wanted to do was curl my palm around my knife. I wanted another fight. I'd had a taste that day, and I wanted more. Needed more.

Human. Demon. I didn't care. I just needed to toss a bone to the dark that was rattling up inside me.

Except I *did* care. Kill a human, and I would be just like the beasts that writhed within me.

But kill a demon . . .

Then I got that nice, sweet hit of the dark. A thick, oily pleasure so intense it was almost sensual. Demon blood. Demon essence. I was *so* all over that.

Too bad there was never a demon around when you needed one.

I was bemoaning that little fact when two short siren bursts startled me. I closed my eyes, gritted my teeth, and turned around to find myself face-to-face with an officer on a bike that wasn't nearly as cool as my dearly missed Tiger. I made a mental note to find time in and around the whole saving-the-world thing to swing by my apartment and pick up my bike.

"Officer!" I said, utilizing the full extent of Alice's perky good looks. "I'm so glad you're here. My car broke down, and—"

"There's no pedestrian traffic on the bridge," he said.

"Right. I know. But—"

"Let's get you back to your car, miss."

Since I already knew that Deacon wasn't back that way, I wasn't particularly happy with the officer's backtracking plan. "No, really, I just need—"

"You're holding up traffic, miss." He glanced down at the holster on my thigh and the strap of leather that formed part of the sword's scabbard. "Am I going to have trouble with you?"

I exhaled, because, really, what else could I do? "Yeah, Officer," I said, flexing my fingers as I imagined my knife. "I kind of think you are."

His eyes went wide. Apparently most hooligans don't admit that they're going to be trouble. Fortunately for my officer friend, I realized that I didn't have to gut the poor guy in order to get my way. As part of my handy-dandy demon-sponge persona, I'd absorbed a whole array of demonesque attributes. Bloodlust, for example.

Get me around the scent of human blood, and I become absolutely ravenous. And not for french fries and a milk shake, either. I'd learned to control it—to a point—but I still wasn't thrilled about having such crazy *nosferatu* tendencies. I wasn't crazy about *any* of these traits, actually, as each and every one tainted my soul.

I might not be a demon yet, but I was no longer fully human. Instead, I was one of a kind, and while I'm all for individuality, trust me when I say that in some circumstances, it sucks.

Still, if you've got it, you might as well use it. And one thing I had was a way to sexually enthrall men. A perk derived from killing an incubus and one that I intended to utilize on my friend the traffic cop.

"Put your hands where I can see them," he said, shifting his stance so that his legs were shoulder width apart, and his hand was on his gun.

"Sure," I said, breathing low, my eyes on his face, as I tried to dredge up my inner sex kitten. I *have* all these traits, but they haven't been part of me for long, and I was still learning how to control and compartmentalize all the swill whirling around inside me.

I lifted my hands, palms out and fingers spread wide. My thumbs rested just beside my breasts, and I let a slow, sensual smile ease across my face. "Like this?"

He swallowed, his Adam's apple bobbing. "Higher," he said, not yet as glassy-eyed as I wanted him. I drew in a slow breath, which had the effect of both centering my power and lifting my boobs. In my old, flat-chested body, that would not be a big thing, literally. Alice, however, had an ample rack, and I was more than happy to use it.

I focused again on his eyes and slowly moved my hands, taking one step forward as I did. I suppose I was technically lifting my hands, but I sure wasn't doing what he asked, because I pressed them softly to his shoulders. He didn't protest, and his eyes now had that glassy lust-filled look. I bit back a smile, the essence inside me preening in satisfaction.

"Is this okay, Officer?" I asked, in my most innocent voice. And then, before he could answer, "How about this?"

I brushed my lips over his, moving my body in closer as I did so. He was tense at first, and I tried to relax. Tried to exude sex and pleasure and sensual allure. I've never been a flirt, much less a flirt with serious mojo, so trust me when I say that it was a new thing for me. But it worked. Somehow, I managed to pull it off. I know because he opened his mouth under mine. He sighed, and the hand left the gun to slide around my waist.

Success flowed through me, all warm and gooey, but I realized then that I didn't know what to do next. Yes, I'd managed to enthrall the man, but so what? I still needed to find Deacon. So what was I supposed to do with *this* guy in the meantime?

His tongue slid into my mouth, and he pulled me tight against him, his growing erection suggesting that he'd be open to pretty much whatever I suggested. Cars rolled by, slowing and honking. Undoubtedly there would be pictures of this cop kiss all over the Internet any second. I hoped the poor guy wouldn't get fired, but since my bigger goal was preventing the Apocalypse, his employment issues weren't my primary concern.

Getting on with finding Deacon was, though, and I gently pushed him away. "Someplace a little more private, maybe?"

"Please," he whispered, the sound low and guttural, with no indication that he was fighting. Nothing to suggest that he wasn't willingly going with the program.

A bitterness welled up in me, and I almost laughed. *Weak-minded idiot.* I frowned, not liking the direction of my thoughts. I was *using* this man, and I scorned him? What was wrong with me?

I almost broke the connection, but common sense prevailed. "Motel," I said. "The Dublin." I rattled off the name of a dive I knew on the other side of the bridge. The place was a hotbed of iniquity, and I'd done more than my share of product trafficking in the dimly lit lobby. At the very least, maybe this guy could bust someone and call the evening a success.

"Now," he said, sounding desperate.

"I'll follow you."

"Here," he said, pulling me closer, displaying a strength I wouldn't have guessed from the skinny frame. *"Now."*

O-kay . . .

Maybe I'd turned the charm on a little too high?

"Soon," I said, trying to ratchet back without cutting him off. "And with privacy."

"Screw privacy," he growled, then reached down to cup my crotch.

I jumped, because I totally wasn't expecting that, and when I did, the connection snapped. "What the fuck?" he said, and I took a step back, reaching for my knife as he reached for his gun.

I got to mine first, pressing the tip up under his chin. "Still," I said. "Don't fucking move."

Fury flared in his eyes, and for a moment I wondered whether he was going to survive this little encounter with Lily Carlyle, über-chick. Because that look in his eyes sparked something in me, and I wanted him dead. I wanted him gone. I wanted his blood spilled on the asphalt, and I wanted to tilt my head back and revel in the scent of it.

Oh God . . .

I took a step back, disgusted with myself, and as I did, his hand closed over the gun. I drew in a sharp breath, my body bracing for the bullet's impact. But it didn't come. Instead, he let out a wail of pain so intense I thought it would burn up my soul.

Out of instinct, I jumped back, my knife tight in my hand, and I saw then the cause of his pain—a sharp blade protruding from his groin. And before I even had time to process that horror, the blade ripped upward, slicing the officer straight down the middle. The halves of his body fell away, revealing a wiry demon crouched behind him, his overlarge teeth forcing his mouth open in a perpetual sneer.

"Bitch," he growled, though I could barely hear him over the squeal of tires and the crunch of metal hitting metal as cars careened to a stop beside us.

"Holy shit—"

"What is that thing—"

"I'm going to be sick—"

"Call 911. Somebody call 911!"

The explosion of voices swirled around me, but I stayed focused on the creature that was lashing out at me with the long, lethal blade.

"Pretty neck on the pretty girl. Cut the neck, take what's around the neck. Take the head, too." Thick, green slime oozed from its mouth as it spoke, and even though I'm über-girl with my powers and my chutzpah, I'll totally admit that I was scared shitless. Because this dude meant business.

And the really scary part? He had nothing to lose. Beneath the thin fur that covered his lanky, wolflike body, the mark of the Tri-Jal burned bright. A snake consuming its own tail.

The Tri-Jal were the worst of the worst. Demons who were little more than attack dogs serving their masters' bidding. So far, I'd only seen Tri-Jal demons with the mark hidden at the base of their neck, beneath a fall of hair. Tri-Jals that still had enough sense of self that they could move among humans.

But this demon . . . Well, it was nothing but a servant, and its master had branded it as such.

So I was wary, yeah.

But I'd be lying if I didn't say that I wanted it, too. Wanted the fight. And wanted to absorb the essence of one of the baddest of the bad.

I lunged, only to find myself immediately yanked backward. I yelped, then heard the leather of the sword scabbard snap. I was free, and I whipped around to find that the demon had brought his buddy to the party—a second snarling, wolflike creature was right behind me, an identical brand upon his chest.

Worse, the new addition to the party had my scabbard, not to mention my sword. *Fuck.*

Not thrilled by this turn of events, I dove to the ground—my left hand closing around the hilt of the gun dropped by the eviscerated officer. I rolled onto my back, and fired two shots in quick succession, managing to nail the new demon right in the gut. The force of the blast knocked him backward, and although I knew that a gunshot wasn't going to kill the demon, it was damn sure going to slow him down.

My first friend, however, wasn't slowed in the least by my attack, and he lashed out at me with his blade. I thrust up with my left hand, blocking it with the gun, the clang of metal against metal harsh against my ears and the force of the blow reverbing down my entire arm.

He thrust again, and I rolled to the side, the point of

his blade landing so close to my ear I could feel the swoosh of air as the steel passed. "The key," he hissed. "Give me the key and keep your neck."

"Fuck you," I said, whipping my leg out so that he fell back. I hurled myself at him, wanting the fight. Wanting the power. And, yeah, wanting to nail the gnarly little beast who'd gone and made an already screwed-up day that much worse. I landed hard on his chest, then slammed the gun against the side of his face, relishing the sound and feel of the skull bones cracking under my blow. He howled, and as he did, I thrust my right hand—and my blade—straight into his heart.

Around me, I heard the cries of bystanders—*Oh God, oh God, oh holy God*—but they meant nothing to me. Though mere feet away, those people belonged to another world. Another world that didn't want this life and didn't need to see it. A world I told myself I wanted to return to, or at the very least wanted to protect, if not for myself, then for Rose.

Except right then I didn't.

Right then, I wanted the dark. The demonic essence. The blackness that had filled the beast, as thick and dark as the familiar black goo that oozed out of him.

And even as life ebbed from him, the dark filled me up. I tried to fight it, because this darkness was beyond anything I'd experienced before. The coarse pain of the Tri-Jal. The sweet pleasure of torment. The need to rip, to rend, to destroy utterly.

I tried to stand, tried to fight, but I couldn't. The world was red.

Raw.

It was pain and fury, and I wanted to lash out and kill. I wanted to fucking destroy, starting with the loudmouthed sheep who stood on the bridge bleating like useless little children. *Run,* I screamed in my head. *Run from me. Run far; run fast.*

I heard the wail of approaching police cars, and through my hazy vision I could see the lights of the four approaching vehicles. An elderly woman in front of me thrust her hand out, pointing at my face, then opened her mouth and screamed loud enough to wake the dead.

And sure as hell loud enough to knock me out of my funk.

I wanted to tell her that I wasn't the scariest thing out there, but I honestly wasn't sure of that anymore. I looked normal, after all, but the dark was in me. And that was pretty damn scary.

The people beside her took up the cry, and, too late, I realized that it wasn't me to which they were point- ing—it was what was behind me.

I whipped around and found myself face-to-face with the demon I'd shot. Needless to say, he was a bit ticked off, and was showing his displeasure by coming at me hard and fast with a sword identical to his buddy's.

My reflexes are pretty damn fast these days, but ap- parently they aren't fast enough. Because even though I thought I'd moved within a split second of seeing him coming, still the sword went straight through me, sliding in just under my rib cage on my left and emerging through the soft fleshy part at my waist on the right side. The demon was close, his stench nearly overpowering, and he wrapped his free arm around me, holding me tight, and pressing so hard against my knife hand that I couldn't move it.

I still had the gun, though, and as we were positioned, the muzzle was pressed hard against his belly. I pulled the trigger, anxious for those few seconds when he would flinch in pain, readying myself to move the second I could.

But absolutely nothing happened.

No bullet, no smell of gunpowder, no horrific eardrum-bursting blast.

Just one measly little *click*.

I was screwed.

More specifically, I was skewered. A human shish kebob entwined with a demon, unable to move, to run, or to fight.

Worse, I knew what was coming—the quick thrust upward with that lethally sharp blade. The same exact thing that had happened to the officer, who was moldering, dead, on the hard concrete surface.

Only me? I wouldn't be dead. Disemboweled. Doubled. Fucked-up for life and in constant, eternal, horrible pain.

But I wouldn't be dead.

And like the thought of burning forever in hell, that scared me even more than the monster holding the sword.

NINE

I tried to struggle, but it was useless, and when I felt the demon's muscles tense, I knew the end was coming. He was too strong, and I wasn't ready for this. Wasn't ready to be thrust into pain and torment and—

Swoosh!

Something hard and fast swooped through the air and tackled us, the force of the blow knocking the demon backward and wrenching his hand free. I collapsed to the ground—the sword still penetrating my flesh, the pain downright agonizing—but I was in one piece, and I figured that counted for a lot.

I rolled to my side, fighting the pain and determined to see my savior. And, yeah, to get the damn sword out of me so that I could fight the son of a bitch.

Of course, my mysterious flying blur of a savior was already down with the fight-the-son-of-a-bitch plan.

Deacon.

I smiled, the pain seeming to lessen simply by virtue of this one thing—one thing out of so many thousands—that had gone a little bit right.

Deacon had come to save me.

He was a man again, or at least mostly. He still had wings, thin yet strong, like the wings of an ancient beast or mythical monster. The rest of the monster was gone, though. At least physically. He might have Deacon's face and chest and coal black eyes, but the rage and fury—the pure intensity—that rolled off this new Deacon was ten times beyond anything I'd witnessed from him before.

He had no sword, and so he'd moved in close to the wolf-beast that had skewered me, tackling him, pummeling him—basically tormenting the creature even though slamming a blade through the beast would have easily done the trick. Deacon didn't want that, though—I could tell.

He wanted the fight. He wanted the fury.

He needed the brutality both to fuel and fight something dark that still grew within him. I understood that well enough; I'd been there myself.

At the moment, Deacon could do whatever the hell he wanted because I was still stuck in place. That was an inconvenience I needed to remedy, and fast, and so I held my breath, then grabbed onto the blade right where it entered my body. The metal was sharper than any advertised Ginsu knife, and it sliced my palms as I slowly drew it out, which had the added benefit of marking the blade as mine.

When I killed with it, the demons would stay dead.

I was *so* going to kill with it.

"Deacon," I yelled, as the Tri-Jal grabbed one of Deacon's wings, then thrust his fist through the thin, strong membrane that formed the actual wing. Deacon roared, low, furious, and full of pain and the promise of payback. I anticipated that he would exhale a gust of fire as he had with Penemue, but none came. Instead, he kicked out, thrusting the Tri-Jal backward before rising high into the air.

I didn't waste any time. I lunged forward, sliding the blade between the Tri-Jal's shoulder blades. It didn't die immediately, and I assumed I'd missed its heart.

That simply wouldn't do.

Behind me, I heard the confused, horrified gasps from the crowd. I also heard the sirens and the voice of the police over the car's PA telling people to move along.

I thought that sounded like damn fine advice.

Then, of course, the voice shifted its attention from the crowd to me. "Drop the sword and step away, hands on your head."

I've never been one for following orders, and I wasn't inclined to start just then. At the same time, I wasn't keen on getting shot.

As I was a pedestrian on a bridge hundreds of feet over the Charles River, my options were limited. Plus, I wasn't keen on leaving the demon writhing on the end of my blade alive.

I told myself I didn't want him to hurt all those nice

people. But that wasn't my sole motivation. It was that hit. The first Tri-Jal had freaked me, I'll admit. But having tasted it, I wanted it.

I wanted the demon to die, so I could have a taste of what was inside him.

And how fucked-up was that?

"Now!" the cop's voice boomed behind me.

But since "now" didn't work with my schedule, I did the next-best thing. I screamed for Deacon. A dangerous option with him balancing on the precipice between man and demon, but right then, I didn't think I had a choice.

For a moment, I feared he wouldn't come. Then he swooped down, his arms out, his body listing precariously to one side to favor the injured wing as he grabbed me and lifted, the movement pulling the sword free. I shouted in protest, urging Deacon back toward the demon. A risky move, since the eager officer had a better shot with us moving forward instead of up. Apparently the cop knew it, too, and he began firing off rounds. One grazed my hip, and from Deacon's sharp curse, I guessed that he'd been hit, too. But for the most part, the shots went wild, a result that I supposed was to be expected under the circumstances. After all, the officer probably wasn't trained to fight pre-Apocalyptic demons. Considering the pudge around his waist, I think catching speeders was more his thing.

"Faster!" I shouted to Deacon, and soon we were going so fast that the world was a blur. I had only my instincts to go on, and so acted rather than analyzed, thrusting my blade out with the hope that this time it would land true, stabbing the beast through the heart. The kind of kill shot from which a demon doesn't recover.

I felt a quick jerk of resistance as the tip of the blade encountered the hard demon flesh. But after that, it slid in like butter. And, yeah, I got the bastard through the heart.

I knew, because I could see the black demonic goo.

More than that, though, I knew because I felt it. That jolt. That delicious, welcome, horrific sense of power that welled within me. *That* was what I was. Power and strength, torment and fury. I was a goddamned force of nature and right then—when I had the power surging within me—that was exactly what I wanted to be.

Do you, Lily? Do you really?

I frowned, ignoring the voice in my head as Deacon carried me and my fast-dissolving cargo up, high enough so that we rose over the bridge's retaining wall and hovered over the Charles. I let the sword tilt downward then, and as a shocked gasp rose from the humans still freaked-out and watching, the body slid from my sword and fell into the choppy water.

I'd expected that would be the end of it.

I should have realized I was wrong.

Where the demon landed, the water seemed to bubble over. Deacon circled back, apparently as interested in the phenomenon as I was. And the folks on the bridge were pretty interested, too. I glanced in that direction and saw a whole crowd gathered against the concrete barrier, their heads bent over, their hands holding tight to cameras and video phones.

And far beneath us, a sight that I was certain would make the nightly news: bloodred water. *All* of the water.

I wasn't the only one who saw it; the confused murmur on the bridge made that clear enough, especially when a few choice words managed to break free of the din: *Armageddon*, *the seven seals*, *portents*, and *though I walk through the valley of the shadow of death, I shall fear no . . .*

The last particularly caught my attention, not because of the words, but the tone. Strong and confident and not the least bit scared. I looked over and saw the priest's collar, and a knot of jealousy tightened in my stomach. He had faith, this man. He had faith that everything was going to turn out all right. That no matter what happened, in the end, he would be okay.

I wished I could share that belief. But I was on the front lines, and I knew there was no such clear-cut answer for me.

I wanted his faith. I truly did.

But I'd seen enough to know better.

Deacon swept us away through the Boston sky, finally tumbling to a halt on the roof of one of the bank buildings, his whole wing tucked closed at his back while the injured one remained open and lopsided. He stood looking at me, tall and stiff, muscles tight with barely controlled energy, his dark eyes flashing with fire.

I eyed him warily, my weapon out and ready. Deacon might have just saved me, but we'd been through that routine before, and the last time, he'd gone from savior to scary in about 3.7 seconds.

I watched as he breathed in slowly, clenching and unclenching his right hand, the muscles in his left arm contracting as well, as he fought to bring himself under control, that fabulous jawline tightening and his strong brow furrowed with effort.

I wanted to move forward, to pull him close and help him find his way back. This was the man who compelled me—who'd gotten under my skin, fired my senses, and made me believe that I had a solid chance to survive the nightmare into which I'd been thrust. The man who had faith that, together, he and I could save the world.

"Lily," he said, his voice as rough as the hand that reached for me, that pulled me close and pressed me hard up against him. "Lily," he repeated, and there were a thousand questions in that one simple name. Questions, and demands, and promises, and I answered them all, taking his face in my hands and crushing my mouth to his.

This was no sweet embrace, no polite lovers' reunion. This was need. This was sex. This was heat and lust and sin and claiming—*Mine,* he'd once said to me, and I wanted everything that simple word implied. I wanted to be had. I wanted to claim, and I wanted to be claimed.

We tumbled backward, landing hard on the rough gravel that covered the roof of the building. My shirt rode up, the rocks pressing into my back, but I didn't care. I wanted it as much as Deacon did—needed it, too, for all the same reasons that he did. A connection. Humanity. A sharing of simple, human pleasures. A way to drown out the demons and remember what the hell it was we were fighting for. Humanity. Love. *Life*.

He fumbled at the button on my jeans, and I reached down, unfastening them, then shimmying a bit until they were down around my ankles. I kicked one foot free but didn't bother with the other. I didn't care. I couldn't wait, and my hands were on his fly, then urging him closer to me as he murmured my name, "Lily, Lily, Lily."

We didn't need the illusion of foreplay—our desire was more than sufficient, but as I urged him toward me—as he thrust inside and split me in two—I felt something warm and gentle flowing through us, counterbalancing our frenetic coupling. I felt it, and I cherished it.

We moved together, a sensual, powerful dance even more ancient than Deacon himself, and when we came, I swear I was amazed that the building beneath us didn't shake with the force of our orgasms.

I pulled him close, finding his mouth, then pressing soft kisses there as I stroked his back, just below his wings.

"Lily," he murmured. "I didn't know. I didn't know if I could find my way back."

"You did," I said, stroking his face. Tears were trickling down my cheeks, and I realized that the demons that writhed within me had calmed, as if they knew that good or bad, they stood no chance against the pull of this man, no chance at all against the two of us together.

"Lily," he repeated, and this time he rolled off me, breaking the contact between us before looking at me. His eyes were as black as always, but I saw a spark in them that I recognized. Life, humanity, a soul.

The wings might still be there, but Deacon was well and truly back.

His shifted, then sat up and tilted his head so that he was gazing up at the vivid blue sky in which dozens of fluffy clouds floated, picture-perfect. Above, it was a gorgeous day, full of hope and light, and I allowed myself a moment of self-satisfaction. Even though it was getting dark and scary down here, Deacon and I had managed to snag at least a little bit of that light.

After a moment, he stood, then refastened his jeans. They hung low on his hips, making him look damn sexy even with the wings, one of which still hung limp from his injury.

He turned away from me, suddenly awkward, and with a start, I realized why—we'd taken each other, claimed each other, and yet never once had he looked into my eyes.

A cold chill ran through me, and I tried to tamp it down. I couldn't, though. Because as much as I wanted to trust in what I felt, it was one hell of a lot easier to trust in what I saw.

And so far, Deacon was showing me nothing.

Again and again, he had pulled away, refusing to let me see the worst of him. Refusing to let me truly understand who he was and what he did, the crimes for which he so desperately sought redemption.

I reminded myself that I trusted him. That I'd been through this mental exercise before.

I told myself not to push. Not when I'd just gotten him back.

I told myself those things, and yet it was hard. Damn hard.

I sucked in a breath, then stepped toward him, my heart breaking a little when he took a wary step back. I slowed, then let him watch as I ran my blade along my fingertip, drawing blood. "Your wing. Let me help."

He nodded slowly, then extended the injured wing, turning his face from me as he did, as if having me tend the demonic part of him shamed him. I moved forward slowly, then held the wing steady. Though fragile in appearance, the membrane was strong, and I traced a bloody line over the rent in the thin skin, then stepped back to watch as the power of my blood did the trick, the injured area knitting together until it appeared as though the wing had never been wounded.

"Thank you," he said.

I took a step back. It was time for answers. He might not want to tell me what was in his head, but he was damn sure going to tell me what was going on. "What happened?" I demanded. "And start at the beginning. With Penemue. What the fuck happened when we were down in Zane's basement?"

"I saved you," he said, his voice harsh. "Or hadn't you noticed?"

I swallowed. "I noticed. And thank you," I added softly. I drew in a shaky breath, remembering that horrible moment when he'd fallen into the pit. "I'd thought you were dead."

He dropped his gaze to my thigh and the blade sheathed there. "You forget what I am, Lily. And falling into hell won't kill a demon."

"Tell me," I said, because I needed to hear it. No matter how much I didn't want to, I needed to hear out loud what Deacon had become—and why.

"I fell," he said. "I fell for what seemed like days, but must have only been seconds. I'd crossed into hell, Lily. Not the darkest pits. Not where Penemue himself had once entrapped me to punish me for my treachery, but still hell. Still dark. And vile. And full of power and possibility."

I pressed my lips together, understanding. I'd felt the darkness within me, too. The lure of power and the promise of possibility. But I didn't want it. The price was too high, the pleasure an illusion. But tempting. So very, very tempting.

"How did you get back?" I asked.

"I changed," he said simply, though I saw on his face how much the admission cost him. "I took back my original form." He closed his eyes, his body fairly rippling with the effort of control. "I let myself slide back into—into *this*."

He nodded, indicating himself, and I moved closer,

then pressed my hand on his chest. I felt it, that spark that always arced between us. "Whatever form," I said, "you're still the same man. You fought your way out once. And you've done it again now."

He tilted his head down, and as he did, he extended his wings to their full span. "Have I?"

"Yes," I said firmly. "You have. My question is why. How?"

"I knew you were trapped," he continued, then moved away so that I was no longer touching him. Only then did he lift his head and meet my eyes. I understood; he didn't want me falling into his thoughts. Didn't want me seeing everything dark within him and within his past. "And although Penemue is too massive to quickly cross dimensions," Deacon continued, "I knew that sooner or later he would manage. He'd burst free and consume you. You'd be alive," he said, "like Jonah in the belly of the beast. And Penemue would again have the *Oris Clef*. He'd use it, and he would rule."

He met my eyes and saw something hard reflected there. "That wasn't what I wanted."

I swallowed, hating the question but knowing I had to ask. "What *did* you want? To keep me safe? Or to get the *Oris Clef* for yourself?"

Something hateful flashed in his eyes, and I winced, knowing that I'd hit upon a kernel of truth.

"I want *us*, Lily. I want what I've always wanted." He took a step toward me, and the air between us seemed to shimmer from the heat of desire. "I want to lock the gate. I want redemption. I want you."

"But?"

He closed his eyes, silently acknowledging the legitimacy of the question. "But there is a part of me—the part I let back in, the part that freed us from Penemue—"

"Yes?" My question came out as a whisper, a breath laced with fear.

"And it wants power," he said, his eyes dropping to my neck, to the *Oris Clef*. "Why do you think I told you to run?"

"Right." I licked my lips, then tightened my hand around the hilt of my blade. Just in case. "And now?"

He turned from me and walked to the edge of the building, his wings folded neatly at his back. The gravel on the roof crunched under his feet, the sound like small explosions in the relative silence. "Now I fight that desire. I fight, Lily, every moment of every day."

I could hear the torment in his voice, and I understood it. I fought too, after all. Every damn day.

We were the same, he and I. Even without a peek inside his head, I knew that. There was darkness in there—vile, horrible darkness—but it grew within me also. And we could do nothing more than cling to each other and hope that we each had the strength to help the other fight. Because our nature was trying to claw its way free. And if the beast got loose before we sealed the gates, we'd be well and truly fucked, and the world along with us.

That, I realized, was what I feared. That somehow the beast really was loose in Deacon, and he would manage to keep it hidden until it was too late for him or for me or for the whole damn world.

He crossed to me, his strides long and determined. "What do you need to trust me? To truly trust me? Must you really get in my head? Is it so necessary that you look upon the vile things that I have done and marvel at the horror wreaked by my hand?"

"No, I—"

But whatever protest I intended to foist was left unsaid, because he pressed a hand to my face, then met my eyes. I felt the hard tug of the vision, and as the darkness that lived in his mind drew me in, I saw him wince but hold steady.

Pain.

So much pain.

And blood.

Dripping down walls; staining tile floors.

And screams so loud and desperate I feared they'd echo in my thoughts forever.

I wanted to run. Wanted to turn my mind back from such horror, but I was compelled to go on. Terrified, but determined to see what he was, finally, allowing me to see.

I was in a corridor, long and dark. A light burned at the end, eerie and yellow. That, I knew, was where I needed to go. If I wanted to see Deacon's past, the things for which he had been denied absolution, I needed to walk through that door.

I hesitated, then moved a single step closer. The

door, it seemed, moved farther away, the corridor appearing to elongate. Another step, and again the doorway moved.

Well, damn.

Deacon, I realized, wasn't quite as open to letting me see what was there as he'd seemed. But now that I was in—now that he wasn't breaking the connection—I was determined to know.

I kept moving. Slowly at first, then picking up speed, finally breaking into a run and hoping that I could outrun his hesitation. That I could make it to the end of the corridor before he managed to extend it so far that I would end up lost in his mind for an eternity.

Down I flew, and though my head knew that I wasn't really running, still I gasped for breath.

I pushed on, even as the walls around me began to weep blood, and the ground beneath my feet became slick with it.

I stumbled, my body suddenly covered with the stuff, and the bloodlust came upon me. I slowed, wanting to sniff it, wanting to taste it. Wanting nothing more than to stay right there, lost in a river of blood.

No.

He was doing this. Maybe not on purpose, but to slow me down. He didn't want me to see. Didn't want me to know.

But I had to, and I raced forward, ignoring my own perverse craving. Because I couldn't stop. No matter what, I had to see what lay beyond that door. Because how could I trust—how could I believe—unless I knew what he really was? What he'd done?

How, I wondered, could I love this man without fully understanding him?

And I did love him. He filled and finished me, and despite everything, in his arms was the only place I felt safe.

Faith.

The voice was small, almost unrecognizable. And I rushed on, brushing it away like a gnat.

Faith, Lily.

I'd reached the door just in time to catch it as it slammed shut. I slid, like a runner going into home, jamming my foot into the space so that the door couldn't latch.

I'd done it, and I stood carefully, not letting the door close, fearful I'd fall. That something would swoop down and attack. That the floor would drop out from under me.

None of that happened.

This was my chance. And as my hand closed around the knob—as my muscles tightened to push the door open—I heard that small voice again. *Faith.*

This time, I recognized it. The voice, I realized, was me.

I hesitated. And then I took a single step back. I let the door fall shut, and I heard the lock click into place.

He didn't want me there, not really. Not yet. When he was ready, he'd tell me everything. Until then, I was with this man. And I held fast to my faith that I was doing the right thing.

About the end of the world and my ability to stop it, I was still woefully unconvinced. But this flower of faith that was truly blossoming within me? Well, I figured it was a start.

TEN

"I can't go in."

"What?" We were standing in front of St. Jerome's Cathedral, a Boston church that predates the Revolutionary War. According to Deacon, this was Father Carlton's parish, and if there were people who knew the details of the father's work, they would be here.

Tourists swarmed around us, cameras clicking as they moved en masse into the building, all oblivious to who and what we were. Understandable, I supposed, as we now looked more or less like your average citizens. We'd taken the more traditionally accepted route off the building, opening the door for roof access, finding the elevator, and taking that noble invention all the way down to the lobby. Actually, we'd taken one small detour before that, popping into the reception area of one of the office suites. I'd distracted the receptionist with claims that her boss, Big

Charlie, had ripped me off. And while she'd repeat-
edly denied knowing anyone named Big Charlie,
Deacon had slipped into the coat closet and stolen a
suit coat to cover the wings that wouldn't, despite all
his concentration, disappear.

After that, we'd been able to move more comforta-
bly through the world, though Deacon did garner a few
lustful stares from women admiring his bare chest under the Armani jacket.

"The church," he repeated. "I can't go in. I'm not
even sure I can go closer. Goddammit," he shouted,
with such sudden fury that a nearby couple with a baby
scurried away, the child tucked protectively next to the
woman's chest.

"I'll go in," I said, though his inability worried me,
suggesting that the demon was far more prevalent than
the man.

"That's not the point," he said, rage and self-loathing
clinging to him like grime. "I try so hard—so fucking
hard—and nothing is goddamned good enough."

"Everything is good enough," I said, stepping close
and pressing my hands onto his shoulders. "Don't you
see why you can't go in? Because of me, Deacon. Because of me and Rose. You let yourself fall back into a
world you hated because you knew that there was no
other way to keep us safe—to keep the *Oris Clef* and
the whole damn world safe."

I drew in a deep breath because, honestly, I was
pissed off. "If that means that you don't get an engraved invitation to heaven, well, then you know what?

I'm thinking that heaven's got its damn priorities screwed up."

He cast a sideways look toward me. "Do you know why I came to the bridge?"

I shook my head.

"To hear them. To hear them and remind myself what I fight against and what I want."

"Who?"

"The demons. The horde. The allegorical horsemen."

My mind twisted, trying to make sense of what he was saying. "Wait. Are you saying it's there? The portal? It's on the freaking bridge?"

"Above," he said. "Where the spires hit the sky. That's where I was sitting, listening to their call. It's tempting," he said, his voice soft, almost melancholy. "It's so damn tempting to do nothing except slide back into what I am, to let myself be absorbed by my nature."

My chest constricted. "I know."

He drew me close, then pressed my back against his chest, his arms tight around me. "I fear I will have to draw upon the dark again to keep you safe. That without the power of the dark, we won't be able to finish what needs to be done."

I feared the same thing. That every step I took toward saving the world was a step toward destroying myself. Each time I fought for good, I became a little bit more bad.

"What if we can't do it?" I whispered. "What if we can't save the world before our nature gets the better of us?"

I expected words of comfort—promises that all would be well. Instead, he simply pressed a soft kiss to the top of my head, and I understood. There were no guarantees. Not then. Not ever again.

I nodded toward the church. "This may not help. They may know nothing about the rumored key."

"It's a risk," he agreed.

"There's something else," I said. "Something else you need to consider."

His brow furrowed. "What?"

"What if the rumors you heard were right? There *was* another key, but it's already been found?" I took a step back and pointed to myself. "*Me.* What if I was the key you'd heard about?"

He shook his head. "No."

"You have to at least consider the possibility," I said. "You can't cling to a vision you saw before I killed Father Carlton." Deacon's vision that he and I would seal the Ninth Gate together had been brutally clear. Moreover, it had meant the promise of redemption for him. Seal the gate, stop the Apocalypse, and gain entry into heaven. A decent trade-off, and one that he'd been striving for, fighting his dark nature as he searched for the woman of his vision, at first believing her to be Alice, then, later, realizing it was me, thrust into the body he'd seen.

But his vision had come before the prophecy kicked in. A cryptic bunch of nonsense words, the prophecy basically said that Prophecy Girl—me—would have the power to open or close the gate. To cause or prevent Armageddon.

Not that anyone had bothered to tell me that. Instead, the demons tipped the scale. They manipulated the prophecy. They made me. They tricked me. And when I killed Father Carlton, I made the choice described in the prophecy. I'd chosen my allegiance. And now, I feared, I was screwed.

More than that, I feared that any vision that Deacon had seen was all shot to hell. After all, visions weren't set in stone. They were a preview of the future, sure. But they could change on a dime.

Deacon was watching me, his expression thoughtful. "Shall we call Gabriel now? Have you go away with him to await the convergence?"

I winced. "Not top of my list, no."

"Then there's no harm in trusting my vision, is there? We have four days. We find the key during that time, and you're safe. We both are."

I nodded, and we simply stood for a moment, him holding me tight and me pressed up close, listening to the beating of his heart. It was the sound of humanity, and somehow, hearing it in the chest of this demon, gave me hope.

"Do they know what's happening?" I asked. "The regular humans, I mean. Like those people on the bridge. The people here, visiting this church. Do they understand?"

"Some," Deacon said. "The rest probably think what they saw was a publicity stunt."

"Not just the ones who saw our fight. I was talking about the world. All the humans."

"Some see the signs and believe," he said. "Some refuse to open their eyes."

"And when they see something like Penemue?"

His mouth curled up in a half grin. "That might convince them. Maybe."

What I didn't understand was why I wasn't seeing Gabriel and Penemue or even Kokbiel around every corner. The demons trying to cut off my head for what was around my neck, the angel trying to take me away, intent on sacrificing me for the greater good.

"Gabriel can no longer take you by force," Deacon said after I voiced the question, his eyes dipping to the *Oris Clef*. "You are protected now by its power. That's how you were able to get away after he had captured you in the chamber. Once you had the *Oris Clef*, his hold on you weakened and broke."

"Oh." That was a bit of good news. And certainly explained a lot.

"He can still try to persuade you to go with him willingly," Deacon added. "Frankly, I'm surprised he has not."

I didn't tell him about the strange illusion of Gabriel's face floating over Madame Parrish. "What about the demons?"

"They're not like me," Deacon said. "Penemue and Kokbiel are massive, cross-dimensional beings that have only become more massive during the time they've spent cast out. They're not so much beings as they are forces of nature, and for them to create a portal to this dimension and manifest takes an act of great power, and always with a counterbalancing effect upon the world."

"Counterbalance?"

"Earthquake, fire, tornadoes. Like I said, forces of nature."

"The earth trembled," I murmured, thinking of the newspaper article and the comment that the Shanghai earthquake was only one of several that had been sweeping the globe. "They're coming," I said.

Deacon nodded. "They are. And I'd guess that Lucas Johnson is, too. We defeated him, and now that you have what he and his master so desired, he'll be back, Lily."

"I know," I said. "And soon."

ELEVEN

The October sun hung low in the sky as I entered the church, its rays bursting through the stained-glass windows and giving the interior an ethereal quality, as if this place existed in some rainbow dimension, where nothing could harm a thing of such beauty. There was no formal service, yet the pews were full, the faithful on their knees, hands clasped in front of them, heads bent in prayer.

Many held rosary beads, and I could hear the low murmur of their Hail Mary's. Some, though, were there only to soak in the comfort of the room, and rather than pray the rosary or cast their eyes upon the crucifix that hung at the front of the room, they were looking around at their fellow worshippers. And, of course, at me.

Me, in my battered red duster, with my black boots, mussed-up hair, and bloodstained tank top. It's a wonder they all didn't run screaming from the room.

Naturally, the moment *that* thought entered my head, that was exactly what happened. A grizzled old man stood up, his coat hanging scarecrowlike on his bony shoulders. "That's her," he said. "The girl from television. She cavorts with demons, she does!"

Heads snapped up. Women clutched their children and scooted backward. Men stood, their faces full of false bravado, hands clenched tight into fists, as if they had even the slightest chance of winning in a fight against me.

"You want a piece of me?" I snapped, a raw fury rising in me. I was risking my sister, my life, my *soul* for these people, and they stepped up to accuse me without even understanding? What the fuck was that about?

The darkness inside me writhed and twisted, urging me to lash out at these fools. These people who didn't understand who I was or what I did and only wanted to wallow in their fear and condemn those who were trying so desperately to save them. "Do you *really* want a piece of me?"

A tall, skinny man stepped forward. "I saw you, too," he said. "But I don't think you were cavorting. I think you were fighting."

I drew in a breath, then released it slowly. Finally, someone who had been paying attention. "I was. I am." I lifted my chin. "That's what I do."

He looked me up and down, his face soft and pudgy, but his eyes sharp and quick. "Hell of a fight," he said. "What are the stakes?"

"Do you really want to know?" I don't know why I stood there, engaged in such an inane conversation. But something inside me told me to stay. To see it through. Not so hard to obey that urge, frankly. At the moment no one was trying to kill me. And that, at least, was a good thing.

Behind him, a few others had gathered, their faces full of curiosity. Many still stood back, clearly not trusting anyone who was fighting on a bridge with two furry wolflike beasts and one Pterodactyl-winged human.

The man looked behind him at the small group, then held out his hand to a petite woman with a baby on her hip. She took a step forward and grasped his hand. "Yes," she said. "We really want to know."

"Armageddon," I said, which set off a riot of voices behind me.

The man clutched his wife's hand tighter, but his eyes never left me. "You lose, and it's all over for us." It was a statement, not a question.

"Yes."

He nodded slowly, as if taking that in, and when he lifted his head once more to look at me, I gasped. Because the pudge I'd seen earlier had vanished, replaced by a warrior's countenance. *Gabriel.*

I gasped, and took a hurried step back, but the man didn't seem to notice.

"Are you going to lose?" he asked, though he spoke in the voice of the angel, his words seeming to come not from him but from the very air that surrounded us.

I shook my head, then lifted my chin. Firm. Certain. "No," I said. "I'm not."

The illusion faded, and the man in front of me was once again only a man. I blinked, wondering if what I'd seen had been real or simply my mind playing tricks on me. In the end, I supposed it didn't matter. Because I'd meant what I said: I wasn't going to lose.

To meet that rather ambitious goal, however, I needed help. "Did Father Carlton have an assistant?" I asked. "Another priest, maybe? Someone he shared information with?"

The man's pudgy brow furrowed. "I don't know. I don't think so."

"He was close to the monsignor," his wife said.

"Is he here?"

The two exchanged glances. "He's . . . He's not well."

"Don't make me spell out how important this is."

The man looked back at his wife, who nodded. "Take her," she said, as a low rumble of protest broke out behind her. To their credit, they both ignored the gripes, and no one else stepped up. They might believe I was a demon out to murder the monsignor, but nobody seemed inclined to step up and do anything about it.

A dark finger snaked through me, contempt for those who came here and sat on their rears and prayed, then didn't lift a finger when they believed that something bad was about to happen. If it was their faith that stilled them, then perhaps my lack of faith wasn't such a handicap after all. I, at least, was taking action.

The man who might have been Gabriel led me into the back of the cathedral, down average-looking hallways that could have been in any office building. I kept expecting us to stop at one of the doors and enter an office, but we kept moving through the building until we finally exited and entered a landscaped courtyard. "Where are we—"

"Through here," he said, pointing to a gravel path. I looked around, suddenly wary. Maybe this guy wasn't on my side so much after all. Maybe he was leading me to the slaughter.

Or, thank you, Miss Paranoid, maybe he was leading me to an elderly white-haired man with skin so thin I could see the blood pumping through his veins.

I drew in a breath, steeling myself. There was no blood spilled, and I was *not* going to let my bloodlust kick in merely from the thought of what flowed within. Simply not happening.

"Monsignor Church," my guide said, shaking the shoulder of the man sleeping in the garden chair. "Monsignor?"

"Church?" I said.

The man actually smiled. "He lived up to his name."

"Is he okay?"

"Old. Very old." He gave the shoulder another gentle shake. "He lives back here. A perk of the Diocese, I guess. He's a little fuzzy in the head, but Father Carlton watched over him." He looked at me, and I forced myself not to react, reminding myself that this man would have no idea who I was or what I did. "I guess now the new rector will step in and take care of the monsignor. Father," he said, bending down close to his ear and speaking loudly. "Father, wake up. You have a guest."

The old man sputtered and jumped, rheumy eyes blinking open as he peered first at my guide, then at me. "Is it morning already?"

"Not yet, sir. I've brought someone to talk to you."

"Is it Missy? She was going to bring a new book today. She reads to me," he said, peering up at me. "My eyes went early. Hard to read. Missy does that for me."

"Missy moved away, remember? Last year. But I think Beth is coming tomorrow to read you another chapter from *The Count of Monte Cristo*."

"Good boy." He patted the man's hand. He turned to me. "Nice of you to come, but I've already been taken care of."

"No, she's—"

"I need you to answer a question," I said, hoping to shortcut this process. "About Father Carlton. About the Box of Shankara."

His head tilted up, those damp eyes suddenly sharp with focus. His lips parted as he looked me up and down. Then he turned to the man who'd brought me this far, reached out, and took his hand. "Leave us, please."

"But—"

"Please, Jeffrey. Go."

"It's okay," I said. "You have my word."

From the look he gave me, I wasn't sure that he was impressed by my promise. But he did what the monsignor asked and left, casting one final look back at us before the path curved out of sight.

"What do you know of the box?" he said.

"I know that we need to find another. Or something that serves the same purpose." I scooted a metal garden chair over, then sat down in front of him. My coat shifted back as I did, revealing the knife strapped to my thigh.

"It is you, then."

"Me?"

He nodded toward the knife. "From Antonio's description of Father Carlton's killer. I thought. And now, I am certain."

"Antonio?" I asked, but I feared I knew. I'd killed Father Carlton, but not all of the men in that room had died. Antonio, I assumed, I'd merely injured.

"He was there. Do you deny the things he said you did?"

"I don't know Antonio. I don't know what he says I did. But I do not deny it."

His face turned hard. "Go."

I leaned closer. "I have to fix it. Don't you see? I have to make it right." I squeezed my eyes together, mortified to realize that I was on the verge of tears. "I didn't know what I was doing. I didn't understand the consequences."

"Bad," he said, his voice starting to lose its focus again. "Bad consequences."

"Yeah. You could say that. Can you help me? Will you help me?"

His head tilted as he looked me up and down. I tried to look innocent and trustworthy, but I'm not really sure that I managed. "They play tricks, you know," he said.

"Who?"

"Demons."

I leaned back, eyeing him warily. "Yeah," I said. "I know."

"Make you walk through fire. Make you suffer. Gotta stand strong. Can't fail. Fail and you burn. Faith, child. Call upon the saints and angels when you have need, but in the end, it's faith that makes you strong."

"I know," I admitted. "And I'm finding it little by little. But right now I need to find the key. Will you help me? Can you help me?"

"Tricky they are, the devils. Come like a beautiful woman. Come like an innocent child. Tell you they need help, they will. Tell you they need to close the gate, when all they really want is to hide the key and keep it open forever."

"That's not me," I said.

He looked up, all confusion erased from his expression. "How do I know?"

I felt the weight of the *Oris Clef* against my neck. And though my head told me not to reveal it, my heart pressed me onward. *Faith. Just have faith.*

"This," I finally said, closing my hand around the necklace. "Do you know what this is?"

He leaned forward, then pulled a pair of glasses from the breast pocket of his robe. He put them on, squinted through the lenses, then gasped.

"You know it?" I asked. "Tell me what it is."

"Temptation," he breathed.

"The *Oris Clef*," I said, ignoring the fact that he'd spoken the utter truth. "Do you know what it does?"

"I've only seen pictures. Sketches. The roughest of descriptions." He reached for it, and I eased backward. "How—"

"It doesn't matter," I said. "The point is I can lock the gate open if I want to. And if I wanted to, I wouldn't care about the Box of Shankara or any other key." I pressed my hand over the necklace. "This is my trump card. Which means that if I'm looking for the Box of Shankara—if I'm looking for another way to lock the gate—it must be because I want to use it, not destroy it."

"Perhaps," he said. "And perhaps it doesn't matter what you say."

"Dammit!" My temper flared, and it was all I could do not to leap out of the chair and shake the old man until he told me what I needed to know. "Do you know what's going to happen if I don't find this key?" I clenched my fists, my jaw tight, trying to rein in my temper. "Just tell me this—is there another key? A physical key? Something I could pick up and hold in my hand?" Something, I wanted to ask, that wasn't me.

"I do not know," he said, then cringed back as if expecting a blow. Dammit all, I'd gone and scared a priest. Which, I'm pretty sure, is way up there on the major-sin scale. Pretty much my only way into heaven was this saving-the-world gig, and so far I was busted flat on that one. Especially if what he was saying was true. Because if he didn't know, then I had no idea who would.

"What about Antonio? The one who helped Father Carlton? Can we ask him?"

"Dead," the monsignor said, then crossed himself. "Run down in the street. Hit-and-run, the police said, but I know that wasn't so. They wanted to make sure. Wanted to make sure no one could follow in Father Carlton's footsteps."

I didn't have to ask who "they" were. *Demons.*

"I'm sorry," I said.

"A good man, he was. Man of God. Wouldn't have helped you, though. Didn't know a thing. Not about that. Not about the other key. About the way to lock the gate up tight." He blinked up at me. "It's coming, you know. Soon the gate will open, and—"

"Yeah. I'm kind of hoping we never get to *and*." I scooted my chair even closer. Any more, and I would be sitting in his lap. "Antonio didn't know, but you do. Don't you?"

"Not much," he said. "I don't know much."

"Will you tell me what you do know?"

He blinked, his expression clouding again. "About what? What were we talking about?"

"The gate," I said. "We need to lock the gate to hell. And I need your help."

"That's what she had, I think. The key. The missing key."

"She?"

"Must have been destroyed when he killed her. That's why he killed her, after all."

My head was spinning trying to follow his thoughts. "Who? What are you talking about?"

"Beautiful, she was. Like you. And there was such a light in her. Light that not even the darkness around her could smother."

I opened my mouth to ask once again what the bloody hell he was talking about, but then I snapped it shut. What he was saying . . . There was something so very familiar about his words. "What happened to her?"

"She came to me. I was her confessor. Traveled all this way from Boarhurst. Said she liked us here at St. Jerome's, but I think she was afraid to go into church near where she lived."

"Why?" I whispered. "Why would she be afraid?"

"The things she saw in her life were bad enough, but she had visions. Horrible visions."

"Of what?"

"Of this," he said. "Of the gate. Of the demons rushing through. And she believed—oh, how she believed."

"In what?"

"In her blood," he said, looking up at me. "She said that her blood would seal the gate."

I blanched. "Her blood? Was it blood—her daughter's blood—that would seal it?" *Please, no. Please, please God, let there be another.*

"Daughter?" He shook his head, as if trying to process the meaning of the word. "No. No, it was an athame. A knife."

"Where?" I said, practically pouncing in my eagerness. "Where is it?"

But he didn't answer. He just shook his head in a manner that suggested everything was lost. "Gone," he said. "Probably got it when they got her. Killed her, you know. I'm certain of it."

"But you said blood. What did you mean by blood?"

"She was afraid, so very afraid that the line wouldn't survive."

"I don't understand. Her line?"

"Her bloodline. It was her daughter. Her daughter who she believed would wield the blade and shut the gate."

I could feel myself grow pale. "How long ago was this?"

I watched as he mentally calculated. "Must have been ten, twelve years ago."

"And the woman's name?"

"Margaret," he said. "Margaret Purdue."

TWELVE

"She knew," I said, pacing in front of the couch in Rachel's new apartment. "Your mom *knew*."

"But what did she know?" Rachel asked. Deacon and I had returned to the pub after my meeting with the monsignor, only to find that both Rose and Rachel were asleep. I'd let them stay that way for a while, figuring that with everything that was soon going to be facing us, they would need the rest. But by four in the morning, I couldn't stand it anymore. We were technically on day three now, and counting down fast. I'd shaken both of them awake, and after coffee and Diet Coke, they were both semiconscious and blinking at me, their faces still soft with sleep.

"Everything. Don't you see? He said the key was a knife, and he learned that from Margaret."

"So my mom actually had the key?"

"I don't know," I said, frowning. "The monsignor

seems to think she did, because he said they took it." I closed my eyes, trying to remember exactly what he'd said. "He said that they must have taken it when they killed her."

"I think he's wrong," Deacon said. He was standing by the window, still wearing the jacket, and the street-light floating in from outside cast him in an eerie glow. "I would have heard. There would have been much rumbling in the demonic community if one of the gate keys had been found and destroyed."

"So that means she didn't have it," Rose said.

"Or it means she hid it," Rachel put in.

"That's exactly what I'm thinking." I reached up to the neck of the clean tank top I'd grabbed from the top of Rachel's laundry basket. I pulled it down, exposing the edge of my bra, and the small tattoo of a knife. "A message, maybe? To let Alice know."

"Alice was only a kid when Mom made her get that tattoo."

"I think your mom was covering her bases. Leaving Alice a clue in case something happened to her. Because she knew it was Alice who would close the gate." At that, I glanced toward Deacon, but his attention was elsewhere. "Or she knew it *looked* like Alice, anyway."

"But that explains it, then," Rose said. "Why they killed her, I mean. We've always wondered about why Alice, and that's it, right? Because they couldn't risk her finding the knife and shutting the gate."

"Yeah," I said, sitting on the coffee table. "I think you're right. But we still don't know why me."

"Does it matter?" Deacon asked. "The reasons don't change the reality. It is you. And there's nothing you can do now to change that."

"I know. I just—" I cut myself off, noticing the way Rachel was eyeing Rose. It was a big-sister look that I was more than familiar with, and I wondered why it was being issued by Rachel instead of by me. "Got something you two want to share with the class?"

Rose tensed up immediately, shifting around so that she was facing forward, hands on her knees. "No. Nothing. I'm good."

Rachel reached over and took her hand. "Tell her."

"It's not import—"

"You told me," Rachel said. "But she's the one who should know."

"Whatever it is," I said. "Tell me." And why, I wondered, did Rachel know and not me? Rose was *my* sister, after all.

"It's just that I know. Why you, I mean. I know why the demons used you."

"Oh." I don't know what I'd expected her to say, but it wasn't that. "How?" As I asked, Deacon moved away from the window, crossing like a cat through shadows to stand beside me. His presence should have calmed me. Instead, it made me more wary.

"From before," Rose said, pulling her feet up and hugging her knees. She still wore what she'd slept in, an oversized T-shirt and loose leggings, and she looked small, fragile, and absolutely miserable. "From when he was inside me."

"Oh." The *he* she referred to was Lucas Johnson, of course. The *he* who had screwed up both our lives. "So what exactly did you learn?" I asked, not at all certain I really wanted to know.

Once again, Rose's eyes darted to Rachel. "Go ahead, honey," Rachel said. "She has a right to know."

Rose licked her lips, then nodded. "I was in there, you know, with him. And most of the time I didn't know what was going on. I was just, I don't know, floating or something. Like when you're half-asleep and things are happening around you and you don't understand what's going on."

"Okay," I said, not the least bit sure what this had to do with me.

"But sometimes he dropped his guard, and I could get a peek inside him." She closed her eyes and breathed in hard through her nose. "I didn't really want to. It was—gross. And scary. And—"

"But you saw something?"

She nodded. "I didn't see so much as *knew*. Like all of a sudden what was in his head was in mine, too."

"What?"

"He made you. Not just as Alice, but as Lily, too." She reached over and squeezed Rachel's hand. "He made you, and then when he and Kokbiel saw the chance to make you the girl in the prophecy, they jumped all over it. I was only a way to get to you. So you'd go after him. So you'd die and all this . . . stuff would happen."

"Back up," I said, suddenly very afraid. "What are you talking about? What do you mean, he made me?"

"Mom," she whispered, as a tear trickled from her eye. "He slept with Mom."

"No," I said, shaking my head and backing away. Deacon's arm went tight around me. "No. He's not. He can't be—"

"He is," she said. "Lucas Johnson's your father."

THIRTEEN

"No," I said, nausea rising in me. "No way. He's not my father. That son of a bitch doesn't have a thing to do with me."

"It doesn't matter," Rachel said, leaning toward me. "I know a little bit about having a family that touches up against the dark. And it doesn't matter. You make yourself, Lily. It's not about who your father or your mother or your asshole uncle is."

But I wasn't listening. I was pacing. My mind whirling, my body hot with the fear that comes with having your entire sense of self shifted. I know a little about that—what with getting dumped into a new body and all—but this was different. Then, at least, I knew who I was at the core, even if the package had changed. Now I wasn't even sure about that.

"I'm not a demon," I said. "I can't be part demon."

"You're not," Deacon said firmly, moving to my

side. "He took human form to be with your mother. You're human, Lily, and you always have been."

We both knew that wasn't really true. The prophecy had changed me, and with every demon I killed, I lost a little bit of that humanity. But I'd always believed I'd started from a clean slate.

Okay, *that* wasn't true either. The old Lily had been far from a saint. I'd do whatever it took to make a buck—steal or deal—but it was always so that I could take care of my little sister. And I'd never really felt a sense of wrong until Johnson had touched her. Before that, it had always been about what was easiest. I'd learned better, of course, yet I was still shying away from the hard choices.

"Does it matter?" Deacon said. "Does it matter where you came from?" He looked hard at me, and I knew what he was thinking. If it mattered that I was demon spawn, then he was screwed, too. Because he'd come from the depths of hell and wanted desperately to have the doors of heaven thrown open for him. So far, he hadn't earned his way in. And I had to wonder—was that because of what he'd done or because of what he was?

If the latter, then I was screwed, too.

"It matters," I said. I moved to the window and pressed my hands against the glass, looking down at the street, now starting to come to life with the approaching dawn. "The creature I hate most in all the world is part of me. His blackness. His vileness. And there's nothing I can do. No way I can make that not be so."

I felt someone step up beside me, and turned to see that it was Rose. She reached out and took my hand. "I know," she said simply. And the soft cadence of her voice shamed me. I might have been born of him, but she'd suffered under him. He'd been in her, too. Physically. Spiritually. He'd raped her, body and soul, and between the two of us, I had to acknowledge that she'd gotten the bitter end of Lucas Johnson.

I looked at her, standing taller and more confident than I'd seen her in a year. She'd survived Johnson's mark, and I couldn't be more proud.

She'd survived, and so could I.

I squeezed her hand, then let go, turning to face the room. "I've been their damn puppet," I said. "The demons. Kokbiel." I shivered. So far, Kokbiel had done all his dirty work through Johnson, and although I'd seen a hefty chunk of Penemue, I had yet to view his enemy, Kokbiel. I can't say that I was looking forward to making his acquaintance.

I breathed in through clenched teeth, thinking about what Kokbiel and Lucas had been doing. "They've been pulling strings since before I was born."

"Lily—" I held up a hand to stop Deacon.

"No. It's okay. I'm just making a point. I've been their puppet," I started again. "But they never expected me to turn, right? To figure out I was being used and start fighting to close the gate? So I got in a solid punch. And they never expected us to get Johnson out of Rose. Another solid punch to the jaw. Now I'm going to kick them in the nuts, and hard."

"Good girl," Rachel said, the corner of her mouth twitching. "How?"

"By finding the thing they don't want us to find." I looked at each of them in turn. Deacon, dark and silent, as he watched me. Rose, moving to settle again beside Rachel, her expression open and curious, her sleep-tousled pink hair standing on end. Rachel, leaning forward, eager to hear and to help.

"The knife," Rose said.

"Right. They killed Alice because they believed she could close the gate. But she couldn't do that unless she had the key to lock it with." I looked at Rose, my prize pupil. "The knife. And that means that the monsignor was wrong. The demons didn't destroy the knife when they had Egan kill Margaret. Because if they had, then Alice would have been no danger to them, right?"

I looked to Deacon, and he nodded in agreement.

"So it still exists," Rachel said.

"The problem is where," I admitted. "The world's a big place."

"But it's not in the world," Rose said. "Right? Because you tried to find it using your arm, and you couldn't."

I had to agree. I was still new to the whole magical, mystery-arm-tour thing, but I'd at least managed to harness how it works. I'd cast out to find the key to lock the gates and discovered nothing. That didn't mean the thing didn't exist; instead, it meant that the thing didn't exist in the earthly dimension.

"So we have to find it," Rachel said. "We have to

figure out how to bring it back from whatever dimension it's hidden in."

"How?" Rose asked.

"A Caller," Deacon said, his expression dark. "We need to find a Caller demon."

I'd had brief experience with a Caller demon not too long after I'd become Alice. Father Carlton had found a repentant demon and used him to pull the key for the Ninth Gate from a nether dimension into our world. My rat fink of a handler, Clarence, had told me that the key would *open* the gate, and I'd naïvely set out to kill the Caller and recover the key, all with the intent of preventing the gate from opening and the hordes from crossing over.

Yeah, right.

But that was over and done. The relevant point was that I knew what a Caller was. After all, I'd killed one, and—

Wait a second. Wait just one single second.

My head snapped up, and I stared at Deacon. "I killed him. Maecruth. The Caller demon. *I killed him,* and that means I absorbed his essence. Holy crap, don't you see? *I'm* a Caller now."

Rose squealed, obviously thrilled with this revelation, but neither Rachel nor Deacon reacted with the level of joy I'd anticipated.

"Hello?" I said. "Remember me? Sponge girl? I killed a Caller. So I can do the calling now."

"It's not that simple," Rachel said. She lifted a shoulder. "Sorry, but I know a little bit about this stuff."

"What do you—"

"Do you know how many Callers there are in the world?" Deacon asked.

"No. I've never bothered to examine the census figures."

Deacon ignored my sarcasm. "Calling is not an uncommon gift," he said. "But in most it lies dormant, because without the training, the gift is useless."

"Oh."

"Callers train for centuries," he said. "It's a grueling process. Painful, even, or so I've been told. And when they graduate, they have a unique skill to augment their gift. But skill is not the same as essence, and I don't think that you absorbed Maecruth's skill when you took his essence."

I was afraid he was right, but I wasn't about to give in so easily. "I could try, though, right? Maybe I did. Maybe—"

"Try," he said. "It can't hurt, and if it works, we're that much further along."

I could tell, though, that he didn't expect it to work and, score one for Deacon, he was right. I spent a good ten minutes trying to get my head around the calling thing, and I got nothing. Maybe I did have the skill, and maybe I didn't. But just then it didn't matter, because have or not, I sure as hell didn't know how to access it.

Damn.

"So what do we do?"

"Exactly what we said," Rachel said. "We need to find a Caller."

"Great. Here I am trying to battle the demons back into the hell dimension, and now I have to go up and ask one for help? They're going to whack my head off, and that's not a look I want for the rest of eternity."

"Maecruth sought redemption," Deacon said. "Surely there are other Callers who share that desire."

"I thought you said Callers were rare," Rachel pointed out. "Sounds to me like the odds are seriously against it."

I sighed. "So we find one, any one. And if he's up for helping us, then great. If not, we'll just have to force his cooperation." The thought of doing exactly that gave me a nice little buzz, actually. A buzz for which I wanted to hate myself, but I couldn't. I was too busy reveling in the black-hearted delight that came with the thought of tormenting a demon into submissiveness. How much pain? I wondered. How much pain would it take to hurt a being who thrived on pain and dark?

I realized with a desperate shame that I wanted to find out.

"How?" I said, hoping my emotions didn't show on my face. "How do we find one?"

"I can ask—" Rachel began, but Rose cut her off.

"We don't need one," she said. "We can find the knife ourselves."

We all turned to stare at her, and she shrank back, apparently appalled by the attention.

"What are you talking about?" I asked.

She licked her lips, her expression unsure. "I was just . . . you know. Just thinking."

"Go on," Rachel said, giving her an encouraging pat on the thigh.

"It's just that Alice had to find it, too, right? And her mom wouldn't want her cavorting with demons, would she?" For that, she turned to Rachel.

"No," Rachel admitted. "That would be the last thing Mom would have wanted."

"Right. So that means that your mom was the one who hid the knife. She created a portal, she put it in, and she left Alice a clue. So that Alice could figure it out on her own and wouldn't need to cozy up to a Caller demon."

"But why not just tell Alice? Or tell me?"

"You were on the wrong side," I reminded Rachel, who grimaced in acknowledgment. "And maybe she was afraid Alice would go wrong, too. Either that, or she was afraid that a demon would get the thoughts from Alice's head before it was time to use the knife." I knew damn good and well that demons existed who could read your thoughts as easily as people read the balloons over cartoon characters' heads.

"So she left a clue," I said. "And the clue was my tattoo."

"It fits," Rachel said. "But where do we go from there?"

"I haven't the foggiest."

"Let's see it," Rose said, and I complied, once again tugging down the neckline to reveal the dangerous-looking dagger that I'd always thought seemed so out of place on such a polished and perfumed body.

"Maybe if you put your hand over it," Rose suggested. "The way you do when the symbols on your arm turn into a portal."

I was dubious, but so far Rose was ahead of the pack with ideas, so I figured trying this one out was worth a shot. I drew in a breath, focused, and pressed my palm over the mark on my breast.

Nothing happened.

I sucked in air, closed my eyes, and pressed harder.

Still nothing.

I opened my eyes and looked at Rose and Rachel, both of whom were staring at me with disappointment. Deacon was back in the shadows, his face dark, his expression grave. "What?" I demanded. He might be fighting to keep his inner demon under control, but right then he was the one who knew the most about this stuff, and I needed him to help, not to be the gorgeous guy who held up the damn wall.

"It won't be your body," he said. "An enchantment. She would have enchanted something. Something she could pass on to Alice if she died before she could share the secret herself."

Okay, I forgave him the moodiness because he was absolutely right.

"So Alice's apartment, then," I said, then glanced up at the clock. It was only six in the morning. Plenty of time to go rip Alice's place apart, then get back to open the pub.

"And we *are* opening," Rachel said, when I commented that we could simply keep the closed sign up all day. "We had a deal. I point them out; you kill them. Better, stronger, faster, remember?"

I remembered. And since we'd already fought this battle—and I'd lost, as little sisters so often do—I wasn't inclined to revisit the issue.

"Fine," I said. "We'll be back in time."

Transportation was an issue, of course. I'd left Rachel's car stalled on the bridge—a fact I hadn't shared with her, but since she'd seen the news footage of our demonic battle, I was pretty sure she'd figured that out—and we'd arrived at the pub in yet another stolen car, now parked six blocks away.

"Taxi," Rachel said. "Steal any more cars, and our luck's going to run out. And while I don't think a jail cell could hold either of you, I really don't think we need to waste the time or the energy getting listed on *America's Most Wanted.*"

Since she had a point, we called for a taxi, which was waiting for us in the front of the pub when we arrived downstairs after a ten-minute delay to let Rachel and Rose change out of their pajamas.

The ride from the pub to Alice's apartment was short, and in no time at all we'd divided the place up, with me in the bedroom, Rose in the bathroom, Rachel in the kitchen, and Deacon in the living room. Fortunately, the place was small.

"It could be anything," I said. "How will we know?"

"It would be something she wouldn't get rid of," Deacon said. "Something with some sentimental value."

"Jewelry?" I asked, carrying her jewelry box into the living room, so I'd have company as I worked.

"Maybe, but doubtful," he said. "Too easy to lose."

"Will you be able to tell?" I asked. "If the thing is a portal, I mean. Can you feel it? Can you sense it?"

"Sometimes," he said, his expression grave. "Let's hope this is one of those times."

Most of Alice's jewelry was early-American flea market, though she also had several really pretty pieces that Rachel identified as her designs. "I should make you toss those," she said. "The company was started with blood money."

I shook my head. "They're good, and they were a gift, and you've started fresh. Did you give them to Alice hoping she'd come back to the black arts?"

"God, no," Rachel said.

"Then forget about it and get back to the kitchen."

She snorted. "Like my mother would put a portal in a cookie cutter." Then her face brightened. "Actually, Alice loved to bake sugar cookies with Mom. Maybe she would," she said, then disappeared beneath the counter, presumably rummaging for kitchen utensils.

I went back to the jewelry box, and even though it pained me to rip such a pretty wooden box apart, I forced the drawers out, peeled up the velvet bottom, and generally inspected every inch of it for hidden compartments. I found nothing.

"No go," I told Deacon. "You?"

"Nothing." He'd been examining the various knick-knacks that dotted Alice's shelves.

I headed back to the bedroom to continue my search. I'd already pawed through all of the dresser drawers, so I started looking at all the books on her shelves. Alice had eclectic reading taste—a hell of a lot more literary than mine—and I carefully pulled down everything from paperback copies of current romance novels to pristine old copies of Dickens and Faulkner. Apparently Alice not only read books but collected them, too.

"There's nothing in the bathroom," Rose said, coming up beside me. "Not unless her mom put a portal in the toothpaste, and Alice hung on to it for a decade." She flopped onto the bed, and I barely moved the books out of the way before she landed on them.

"Careful! These things are expensive."

"Really?" Her nose crinkled. "Why?"

"They're rare. Collectible. And probably worth a fortune."

"Yeah? Huh." She turned away from the books, then shoved herself off the bed. "Guess I'll go help in the other room. So far, this has been a total—"

She cut herself off, turning to me with wide eyes.

"Rose?"

She didn't answer, but crossed to me in three long steps, then grabbed the front of my shirt.

"Hey!"

"This," she said, jabbing my tattoo with her index finger. "I told you it was familiar."

"What are you talking about?" I asked, willing my-self not to get my hopes up.

"In Rachel's apartment—in Egan's old apartment—I saw a book. Old like those. And that sword was on the cover." She looked up at me, her face bright with anticipation. "That's it. I'm absolutely certain."

FOURTEEN

"I told you," Rose said, shoving a battered, leather-bound book into my hand. "See. Right there." She tapped the cover and the faded image of a dagger. "It's the same," she said. "I told you it was."

I looked from Rachel to Deacon. "She's right."

Rachel took the book and started flipping through the pages. "They're blank," she said. "But look at this." She turned back to the flyleaf. There, in neat print, was an inscription: *For my darling Alice. May you always have the courage to do what is right.*

"Egan took it," Rachel said. "He must have, because I've never seen it before, and I know Alice would have shown me. He was the executor of Mom's will. He had the keys to her house. He took it, and Alice never even saw it. Sleazy, horrid bastard."

I seconded the assessment, then gently took the

book from her and handed it to Deacon. "Well? Are we right? Is this some sort of doorway?"

He held the book tight between his hands, then turned to face me. "I think we've found it."

I practically sagged with relief. "So what do I do? Go in, right? Go in, get the dagger, and we just have to use it. Close the gate, lock the damn thing up tight, then we're done. It's over. It's over and we're safe. The whole freaking world is safe."

"First things first," he said gravely. "How do we get in?"

That was a question to which I had no answer, but I was damn well going to find one. "Put my hand over the inscription?" I asked. "That's how it works with my arm."

"Try it," he said.

I did. Nothing happened. Nothing except me feeling a bit like a fool, as if I were in court swearing on a Bible or something.

"An incantation?" Rachel asked.

I groaned. "Great. Something else we have to figure out."

"Blood," Rose suggested. "Isn't it always about the blood?"

The kid had a point. I pulled out my blade, prepared to slice my palm. Then I stopped, suddenly afraid. "The last time we went into a portal, we came out over a week later. What if that happens this time? I'd be sucked in and come out after the convergence, and the whole thing will be a done deal."

"No anchor," Deacon said.

"What?"

"We went in together, so there was no one holding you back, anchoring you to this dimension, this time frame."

"Oh." I hadn't even known that was necessary. "So without an anchor, you're screwed?"

"Not usually. Usually you come back about the time you leave. But Penemue, Kokbiel, those guys are powerful demons. They may not be able to manifest easily, but they exist across dimensions, and they can fuck you up."

"So you're saying it'll happen again."

"Without an anchor, I don't see how you could avoid it."

"Rachel?" I asked, knowing the answer would be no.

"Not strong enough."

I nodded. "You, then."

"I don't want you going in there alone," he said.

"Under the circumstances, I don't think I have a choice."

Rachel glanced sharply at the clock, then frowned. "I didn't realize we were at Alice's for so long." She gnawed on her lower lip. "We're supposed to be open now, and—"

"It's okay," I said. "We'll tell you what happens." I met Deacon's eyes and sucked in a deep breath for courage. "One way or the other, we'll know pretty quick if this works."

She gave me a quick hug, then pulled Rose into an

even longer one before kissing her forehead. "It's going to be okay. You hear?"

Rose nodded, but her smile seemed forced. "This won't even end it, will it? It's never really going to end."

I frowned. "What are you talking about?"

"Even if we stop the horde coming through the gate, the demons can still come, right? I mean, there are demons here now, so there must be other ways in."

I met Deacon's eyes, and he nodded. "Those who practice black magic can open a portal to pull a demon through. But it's hard, and no more than one or two can cross at a time. This, though . . . This would be a flood of millions."

Rose nodded and hugged herself. "I just want it to be over."

"I know," I said, wishing I could make that come true for her. "Believe me, I know."

Rachel came up and gave her a hug. "You need me, I'm right downstairs."

"It'll be okay," I said, taking Rose's hand. "Go."

"Right. I'll be down there doing my job. Scoping them out. Eavesdropping. Figuring out who's about to stir up trouble."

I reached for her arm. "Be careful," I said. "Don't do anything stupid."

"Right back at you," she said, then swept through the doorway. I could hear her footsteps fading down the stairs before the door clicked shut. Then it was just the three of us. Three, and the book.

"Ready?" I asked.

"Be careful," he said, lifting his left arm, and nodding pointedly to the hand that was no longer there. "Remember the acid?" He'd lost his hand trying to find a hidden component of the *Oris Clef*, and it had only been by virtue of the fact that he'd been there to warn me that I hadn't later suffered the same fate.

"I think it's okay," I said. "Alice's mom would have wanted Alice to find it."

"Alice," he said. "But not anyone else."

Point taken. There could be traps. And even though I might look like Alice, I didn't know her history with her mother. If there were secrets between them that would help her navigate an obstacle course, I was woefully unprepared.

"Guess I'll find out," I said, positioning the knife. "At least, I hope I will." I pushed the tip of the blade into my flesh, drawing a thick drop of blood. Deacon had put the book on the table, open to the inscription, and now he held on to the wrist of my knife hand. I waited, fearful this wouldn't work, and at the same time afraid that it would. It's a queer feeling being sucked through a portal, and even though that suck could lead to saving the world—and myself—I still didn't relish the thought of that freakish tug around my middle.

And, I thought, after standing there bleeding for a good thirty seconds, apparently I wasn't going to be feeling it that day.

I spoke too soon. The words were barely out of my head when I felt the yank. A sharp tug near my navel, then—*Oh dear God, help me*—I was plummeting through space, sucked into the vortex that was emerging from the simple book on the table. Color seemed to swirl around me, and I lost all sense of place and time. I'd gone through portals before, but always to someplace on the earth. Never before had I traveled to another dimension, and I honestly wasn't sure what to expect.

Or, for that matter, if the journey would ever end, because it seemed to go on and on and on, and just when I was certain that this was all an elaborate setup to trap me here in neverland, I landed with a hard thud on a glassy black surface. A room, actually, and it was all black. Solid, but with sharp edges. Like lava cooled smooth, then chipped away to make planes and edges, as smooth and sharp as glass.

I saw my own image reflected at me from every surface, my face illuminated from some unknown source. What I didn't see, however, was a dagger, and I immediately looked toward the walls, my eyes searching for the remnant of the vortex through which I could travel back. Because I had a strong feeling that I didn't want to be there. That this black room was danger. That it was death. Or, at least, as close to death as I could come.

There was no tangible basis for my fear, and yet it bubbled inside me anyway, and I wanted out of there. Wanted out so much that I started to move back toward the vortex, now little more than a glowing pinprick in the far wall.

I reached it, and as I stretched out my hand toward it, a face emerged from the wall like a plaster sculpture, formless at first, then gaining shape.

Gabriel.

Terrified, I jumped back. Or, rather, I tried to jump back. I don't know how he managed it, but he had my wrist, his fingers tight around me, and I could feel the power that was this being, the raw energy of which he'd been made manifest.

Deacon, it seemed, was wrong about that whole "Gabriel can't hold you with the *Oris Clef*" thing.

"Please," I whispered, because I didn't know what else to say. "Please."

You dare to beg?

His voice, low and steady, filled my head though not the chamber.

You, who would sacrifice humanity out of fear.

I closed my eyes, shamed because he was right. Because I did fear the torment. I would burn. Dear God in heaven, I'd burn for eternity. "You ask too much."

I do not ask.

And even as he spoke, I felt another jerk, and we were gone from the room, gone from the black glass, moving instead through a misty, smoke-filled world. Noxious fumes surrounded us, burning my eyes and making breathing difficult. Pillars of scorched concrete and steel reaching up toward a smoke-filled sky. And beneath our feet, the bones of those who had succumbed to the horror.

Hell, I thought. The angel was taking me to hell.

Except I knew this place. This wasn't hell. It was Boston.

I could feel the angel's presence behind me. His disgust at all that lay before us. And, yes, at me.

You would let this happen?

I couldn't think. I couldn't process. I stood there, useless, as the ghostly images of people raced past. A group, all fleeing in terror. One fell. A child. And before the group could turn back, the child was pounced upon, the demons digging in, making a meal of the innocence.

A harsh cry pierced the air, and they all turned—demons and humans—toward the sound. Two figures stood there, one lithe with dull black hair and listless green eyes. A familiar face that had seen horror all too often. *My face.* Or, at least, the face that looked back at me from the mirror.

Beside me stood a woman, thin and athletic, with shocking pink hair and an expression that welcomed the kill. She held blades in both hands, and she spun them, the smile that crossed her face one of cruel anticipation. She spoke, and though I couldn't hear her words, I knew she was egging me on. Time for fun. Time for the kill.

Rose.

This. This was what she would become.

Come with me, Gabriel urged, his voice harsh, yet somehow also gentle. *Come with me, and you can stop this.*

I swallowed, terrified of what I saw, of what I knew could come to pass. My mind whirled; my head filled with those dark images and the expression of cruel delight on Rose's face.

But what he asked of me—oh God, what he asked . . .

"Please. I need to think. I need time."

There is no time. There is only—

But I didn't get to find out what the *only* was because I was jerked backward, landing with a hard thump on the obsidian floor. Deacon stood beside me, his face hard, his eyes red with fury. "He isn't really here," he said. "He is an illusion. He can't take you. He can't hurt you."

She will come with me, Gabriel said, and though he wasn't there, he seemed to fill the room, his body huge, the warrior tats on his face emphasizing the anger in his eyes.

"She does not need to die." Deacon's voice rose with fury, and his wings burst free, ripping the shirt so that it hung in tatters around him. "There is another way."

You risk all even by searching. Come with me, Lily. Come with me and do what must be done.

I licked my lips, torn, but it was no longer in my hands. Deacon snatched me up and barreled back toward the vortex. I felt Gabriel's tug as he tried to keep us there, but Deacon was right; he couldn't manifest, and without form, his strength wasn't sufficient to overcome Deacon, especially in the height of his fury.

I felt a sharp *snap* as we burst free of Gabriel's grasp, then rocketed the rest of the way through the swirling mist that made up the vortex, finally bursting through on the other side, landing in a tumble on Rachel's couch. Landing so hard, in fact, that we knocked it backward.

I leaped upon him, a thousand emotions swirling inside me. "Are you crazy? Why did you come? The time thing," I shouted, my fists pounding into his chest. "We could have missed it. We could have lost everything."

I stopped pounding, and he pressed me close, my face against his bare chest, the tattered shirt having fallen away in the vortex. He was trembling from the effort to control himself, and his voice came out a growl, a low rumble that seemed to echo through my body. "It's not too late," he said. "Gabriel's wrong. There's another way. A way for both of us. Together, we'll shut the gate."

I closed my eyes and drew in a shuddered breath, because of course he was right about what was troubling me. It wasn't only the potential for lost time that had thrown me into turmoil; it was what I'd seen. What Gabriel had shown me. And what I feared that I had no choice but to do. Not if I wanted to save the world, and my sister, Rose, along with it.

"You still shouldn't have taken the risk," I said, because I was rattled and needed to pick a fight.

"You were in trouble," he said simply, and I felt his muscles clench, heard the firm cadence of his voice. "You were in trouble, and I couldn't stand for that."

"Me being in danger? Or you potentially losing your chance for redemption?" Because his vision had been clear. Close the gate together, and he would be redeemed. I manage that on my own, and no matter what good Deacon had done—no matter what help he'd been to me—Deacon was pretty much screwed on the absolution end of things. To my mind, that pretty much sucked. But no one had asked my opinion.

"Both," he said, unabashedly honest. He drew in a breath, his face and muscles tight, fighting for control. "I protect what's mine, Lily."

I thought of Rose and closed my eyes. "So do I," I whispered.

Edgy, I pulled out of his arms, then turned around and yelped. Because I found myself standing face-to-face with Morwain.

"Mistress," he said, completing a head-to-floor bow.

"What the fuck?"

"I called him," Rose said. For the first time, I realized she was in the room, too. She'd been curled up in a chair by the window, and had stood, her expression worried. "Deacon saw. Into the portal, I mean. He could see Gabriel. Or sense him. Or something." She looked to Deacon, as if he could fill in the explanation, but Deacon only nodded. She waited a beat and turned back to me. "But we knew he couldn't go help you. Because of that whole time thing. And I remembered what he said," she added, nodding to Morwain. "And so I called him, and—"

"You trusted a demon to anchor us?" I spoke to Rose, then rounded on Deacon. "You let her? Are the two of you nuts?"

"Mistress—"

"No," I said, unsheathing my knife and pointing it at him. "Just, no."

He bowed his head and took two steps back.

"We didn't think we had a choice," Deacon said, casting a dark glance toward the still-open book.

"And I was watching him the whole time," Rose said, tapping the blade of her knife lightly against her hand.

"Great," I said. "That makes me feel so much better." I cocked my head toward Morwain. "I'm going downstairs. Do something with him, will you?"

I knew I was being moody and unreasonable, but considering what Gabriel had shown me, I thought I had a right to be. I left them to deal with the demon in the living room, then went down the stairs to the pub. The two televisions mounted to the wall were tuned to news channels, and the announcers were outlining the various freakish things happening all over the globe. I frowned, wanting Rachel to turn it off, but I figured that would cause a riot. Most of the patrons in the bar were looking at the televisions with expressions of smug anticipation. And, honestly, I wanted to smash their little demonic faces in.

Rachel looked at me curiously, obviously anxious to know what had happened with the book, but she didn't ask questions. Instead, she pulled me a Guinness, then passed it to me with a sympathetic expression. I slid into a booth, leaned back, then silently surveyed the little kingdom over which Rachel and I ruled. A kingdom filled with demons. Demons who were, even then, casting curious glances my way. Some looked at me with fear in their eyes. Others with hate.

I thought of Jarel. There were badasses in there, all right. And some of them wanted to lay me out. Some of them were vile. Dangerous. Utterly despicable, and they'd been coming to this pub for centuries.

The protections that Rachel described had protected the family and, I assumed, the place itself, and I tried to imagine what would happen if there were no protections on the pub. Would it even be standing? I doubted it. Just as I doubted that any of Boston would survive the coming hordes. Not Boston. Not the people in it. Not Rose.

I pictured the corpses that Gabriel had shown me, black and charred. The child upon whom the demons had fallen. I closed my eyes and tried to block the image, but it wouldn't go. That was what they were facing, the humans who dared to cross the demons once they covered the earth like locusts.

And no matter how much I told myself that I could stop it if I stepped in to be the queen, I knew that I couldn't. Not really.

Even if I could retain some sense of self—and that was one big, hairy *if*—who was to say that every demon would follow my rule? Some would seek to depose me. Some would flat out defy me.

And in the end, humanity would die.

Die, and suffer.

I took a long pull of Guinness, wondering if I numbed my body now, would the feeling last for eternity? Because I knew what I had to do. I didn't want to. I was fucking terrified.

But when I closed my eyes, I saw Rose standing there, a blade in her hand and an expression of delighted anticipation on her face.

I knew that I had no choice.

I saw Deacon coming in from the back, his long strides bringing him toward me. I slid out of the booth and moved in the opposite direction, away from Deacon and toward the front door of the pub.

He caught me only moments after I had slipped outside, his hand closing over my elbow.

"Don't," he said, his expression full of dark fury and deadly purpose.

I jerked my elbow free. "Don't what?"

"Don't do what you're thinking of doing."

I turned away, not wanting to see the disappointment in his eyes. Or the fear. "I have to." I tried to push past him back into the pub, but he grabbed me, then shoved me up against the rough brick wall, his body pressed close.

"No," he said, his voice as tight as a wire. "No, you don't."

"Let me go."

"Tell me you're not giving up on this. On us."

I didn't say a word, and I watched as something akin to fear flickered over his face.

He backed away, his muscles going slack, his body suggesting defeat even though his eyes still burned with purpose. "Dammit, Lily, is this really what you want to do?"

"What do you think?" I hissed, wanting to shove away, to hit him. Wanting to claw and fight and draw blood just so the pull of the dark would take me down, down, down, and I wouldn't have to think anymore. Because I was tired of thinking. Tired of plotting. And no—no, I didn't want it, but what choice did I have?

"Find the key," he said, understanding me though I hadn't uttered a word.

"It's gone, Deacon. Don't you get it? We found the book—we found where Margaret hid the knife. And it's gone. Poof. Gone. Just like that." I snapped my fingers. "And do you know what *gone* means? *Gone* means that I'm screwed. *Gone* means that if I want to save Rose, I have to—I have to—" I bit the words off with a curse, unable to say it out loud. "Fuck," I said instead, then stalked toward the door.

This time, he let me pass, which was a good choice on his part, as I was gunning for a fight. I marched across the public area, then through the kitchen and into the back. I weaved my way through the old stone corridor until I reached the heavy metal door that led to the alley. I pushed through it, then sucked in a lungful of air. Even in the afternoon, the alley was dark, hidden in perpetual shadows. Once, the place had creeped me out. Now it felt good. It felt like home.

I leaned my back against the filthy brick wall and scoured those shadows, searching for any creatures that might be looking to rumble. I saw none and had to wonder what was wrong with the local demon population. Wasn't there some big demon crime boss desperate to take my almost crown away? Some sick fuck of a demon who wanted my immortal head mounted on his wall? Somebody who'd step up to the plate and let me kick the shit out of him, then slide my knife deep inside. Because damned if I didn't want a nice solid shot of the dark right then. The more the dark absorbed me, the more likely I was to pick the *Oris Clef*.

My fingers closed over it, and I felt a raw energy surge through me. A hint of the power it had to offer. I sighed, welcoming it. I might not want it—might not believe I could control it—but at least it didn't terrify me the way the thought of going with Gabriel did.

Pain. Forever.

Honestly, that couldn't be good.

I closed my eyes, squeezing back tears, because I knew I had to do it. I'd seen what would happen. To the world. To Rose.

I didn't have a choice.

And still I feared that when the time actually came to act on that choice, I wouldn't be able to go through with it.

The door crashed open again, and Deacon emerged, dark and foreboding and focused on only one thing. Me.

"Whatever you're thinking, Lily, you can't do it. The knife is still out there. It's not gone, Lily. Margaret would have ensured that it was there—somewhere—for Alice to find."

"Yeah?" I said, the tears that had been welling now spilling out of my eyes. "In case you forgot, I'm not

Alice. I don't know where the knife is, and I don't know what to do to find it."

I squeezed my eyes and clenched my fists so hard that my fingernails cut into my skin. "You did it for nothing," I whispered. "You gave up a chance for redemption for nothing at all. Because I can't help you." I reached out and pressed my hand to his face. I wanted to feel him. Longed for more than just the rough stubble of his beard upon my hand. "We're both screwed. You're smart. You have to know that. So why do you care so much?"

"Why do I care?" he growled, stalking forward until my back was pressed against the wall, and I couldn't move without generating friction between our bodies. "Why do I *care*?" he repeated. "After all this, can you really be that much of a fool? Do you not know the way you affect me? Did you not see? You're freedom for me, Lily. Freedom from the dark. With you, I can pull it back. I can control it. I can fight it."

His hands pressed against the wall, only inches from my face. "You're mine. Lily," he said, his breath brushing my hair. "It's not about redemption anymore, Lily. It's about you. And I'll not have you sacrificing yourself. Not like this. Not when there's another way."

"I don't believe there is another way," I said. "And I do understand."

"You're wrong," he said. "And trust me when I say that you don't understand. You couldn't possibly."

And with that, he moved his hand from the brick and pressed it to my face, all while looking deep in my eyes. I wasn't expecting the contact, and the *snap* of connection startled me. I tried to look away, but he breathed a single word—*No*.

And then I was in.

"You wish to understand?" he said. "Follow where I lead."

"No!" I screamed. "I've seen it already! I felt it. I lived it!" And I didn't think I could bear it again.

But he wasn't listening. He took me down, down into the depths, the heat. The pain.

The flesh roasting, curling up off the bone. The animals, gnawing—ever gnawing—at the bodies of the living. Splinters, shoved into skin and eyes and tender places. Bugs crawling beneath the flesh, worms living within. Rotting. Acid. Burns. And the stench and cry of the damned all around.

It was worse than before, as if that were even possible, and I realized that what I'd experienced with Penemue had been what the demon himself experienced. Not pleasure—because how could that word ever apply?—but a pain that he commanded, brought into himself, and reveled in.

Oh God, oh God, he'd soaked up the pain. Craved it. Wanted it.

And Deacon feared and despised it, and he'd suffered all the more for it. Even as I did now. Even as I suffered though I was hiding behind the protection of Deacon's thoughts.

He wasn't letting me out. He was forcing me to watch.

And so I did the only thing I could—I screamed and I screamed and I screamed.

I don't know how long I was out of the vision before I stopped screaming. All I knew was that my skin felt raw, as did my throat. My eyes ached, and the scent of burning flesh clung to me. I curled up on the asphalt, my knees up against my chest, my body shaking as I tried to catch my breath. As I tried to tell myself that I could handle that. That if I had to, I could step up to the plate and endure that suffering forever.

Oh dear God in heaven, I was such a freaking liar.

"I deserved that, Lily," Deacon said, the self-loathing in his voice as thick as oil. "For the things I did, I deserved it for one hell of a lot longer than I suffered it. But you don't," he said firmly. "You don't deserve it at all."

FIFTEEN

I lay there, trembling, trying to fight back the fear—
the horrible knowledge that the thing that I should
do—that I *needed* to do—this thing that could save
the world—absolutely scared me to death. I'd felt it.
I'd *been* it. And I didn't see how I could possibly endure it.

I hadn't even been in Deacon's head for five minutes, and I felt destroyed, as if my body had been
ripped apart. As if I'd never be whole again.

How could I do anything but fight against that possibility? How could I do anything but run?

I hugged my knees and rocked, hating my own cow-
ardice but unable to deny the sharp teeth of my fear. I'd
faced killers and rapists. I'd faced demons. I'd thought
that I knew fear.

I'd been wrong. Fear hides until you become com-
placent, then it jumps out at you. It sinks its teeth into

you. And it takes away even the tiniest hope that maybe, possibly, you'd been working your way up to doing the right thing.

I couldn't. God help me, I couldn't.

"Dammit, Lily," Deacon said, his tone as hard as his eyes. "You don't have to." He reached a hand down for me. "We just have to find the knife."

But as that tiny kernel of courage had left me, so had my belief in miracles. And I knew that it would take a miracle to find that knife. Or, at least, to find it in time. Night was already starting to fall, and soon we would have only two days left. Two days until the end of the world.

Two days until I capped off my rather spectacular array of failures with the biggest one of all.

At least I was consistent, right?

"Take my hand, Lily," Deacon said, holding his right hand out for me.

I hesitated, but honestly, the time for self-pity was over. I either needed to go all out with the demon-queen plan (not), put on a white nightie for my sacrificial debut (big, fat, scary not), or get off my ass and look for the one thing in the whole universe that could save me. We had two full days still, right? And that's two entire lifetimes for some insects, right? Surely I could find one stupid knife with two lifetimes at my disposal.

I took his hand, feeling a little slaphappy. And apparently a little shaky still, because as I stood, the earth seemed to rumble and shake under my feet.

"Earthquake," Deacon said, and I realized it wasn't me after all. He held me close, then moved us into the doorframe.

"Penemue?"

He nodded. "That's my best guess."

"Is he out?"

Deacon hesitated, then shook his head. "No. It would take a massive quake to free him."

I licked my lips. "Then that's probably coming."

"I think we can count on it."

I drew in a breath, then nodded firmly, gathering my resolve. "Okay, then. Positive thinking. We find the knife. We lock the gate. And then I'm buying the whole damn world a round of Guinness." I cocked my head and frowned. "Where do we look that we haven't already?"

He was about to say he didn't know—I was absolutely certain of it—when Rose burst through the back door, gesturing frantically. "It's Rachel," she said, shoving a sword into my hand. "Hurry! Lily, please hurry!"

We raced through the pub, Rose leading the way, breathlessly telling us about how Rachel had stepped outside to clean up some trash that someone had left on the sidewalk right in front of the pub.

I could guess the rest. The pub itself was empty, not a demon in sight. And yet I could see a maelstrom of motion through the leaded-glass windows. She was out there, with the demons. And the demons were pissed.

"They learned," I said, sprinting toward the door and

pulling it open. "Didn't they? They realized what she was doing. That she was pointing them out to me."

"I don't know," Rose said. "I don't. All I know is that they all got up after she went out."

I was peering out on them, at the manifest horror of a demonic mob. And what I was seeing wasn't about killing Rachel. It wasn't about taking her out of the equation so she couldn't point me at any more demons.

It was about payback. About making her suffer. Not a fast kill, but a slow, painful nosedive into oblivion. And only when she'd suffered enough would they end it for her.

At least a dozen demons made up the mob, and as the crowd shifted and turned, a living mass of writhing evil, I saw the demon in the middle reach down and draw her up. Her face was pale, and her eyes scared, but she was alert, and her expression was completely "fuck you"—and right at that moment I couldn't have been prouder if she were my own sister.

As I started to race forward, the demon grabbed an arm, offering her other limbs to three cronies, and they yanked on her as if they were going to quarter her right there in the streets of Boarhurst. Honestly, I wouldn't have put it past them.

Deacon's hand closed tight on my shoulder, pulling me back. *"Think,"* he said. "That's Cryonic," he said, pointing to the tallest demon. "He's the one I bought the paralytic from," he said, referring to a rather unpleasant episode where my entire body had frozen up after being shot with the damn stuff. "I'd wager the damn gate key that if you rush in there to save her, he'll jab you with the stuff. We can't afford to have you out of commission, Lily. Not now."

He nodded toward the screaming mob, jeering and cheering, urging the four attackers on. "One quick throw of my knife, and it's over for her. She's out of the fight, and you're safe. She'd want that, Lily. She'd want you safe."

I turned to him, appalled, wondering which Deacon I was speaking to, the man or the demon.

"No," I said. "No way. She doesn't die. Not on my watch. No way. No *fucking* way."

He hesitated a moment, then nodded. "All right," he said, his voice all calm control. "We fight."

Darkness rippled across his features, and I welcomed it, even though I knew what it was. It was the same darkness that was welling in me—wanting the fight. Welcoming it despite the insane odds.

Deacon had said he feared we couldn't save the world and keep our humanity, and right then I was afraid that he might be right. I might not even be able to save Alice's sister and fight back the lure of the demons.

But I had to try. If I didn't, the demons within had already won.

"Now," I shouted, and as I raced forward, Deacon threw that blade, his aim true. But not for Rachel. No, he was aiming for Cryonic. And although the demon shifted left, the blade still sliced him, the force of that razor-sharp blade slicing off the demon's elfin ear.

The beast howled, giving Rachel's arm a hard jerk, but not so hard that it came off. The other three demons kept hold of her, and as Deacon rushed into the fray, fighting back the demons that had broken free of the mob and were lumbering forward to stop him, I bulleted forward, brandishing the sword and cutting down everything in my way that even freaking moved.

"Call Morwain," I shouted to Rose. "He wants to prove his worth to me, he can damn well start now. And you," I added, throwing the words over my shoulder as I raced forward. "You stay out of this fight."

"Lily!" Rachel's voice was pure anguish, and I saw that her three captors were positioned to rip her apart. I dove, leading with my blade, and cut one of them down at the ankles. He stumbled, dropping her, and throwing his compatriots off balance. The confusion gave me the opportunity to rush farther into the fray. I wasn't concerned about fighting skills or my training or any of it. All I wanted was the kill, and I lunged forward, skewering the other demon who'd had Rachel by the arm. He dropped her, and she hit the asphalt hard. As she did, the demon glanced down, taking his eyes off me for just a split second.

That was one second too long.

I slashed out with the blade. I connected. And I cut off the smug son of a bitch's head.

After that, things got crazy. Well, crazier.

Rachel was on the ground, and the demons were on me, and I was kicking and thrusting and hacking for all

I was worth, landing some sweet, solid blows, but no kill shots. Nothing that got me nice and juiced up, and dammit, I needed the hit, the strength.

Needed, and wanted.

Beside me, Deacon was lost in the battle as well, wild, his demonic nature, I feared, taking over.

But at least it was killing. It might not be on my side—might only be looking out for itself—but so long as he was in the fray and killing the bad guys, I could deal. For now—until we got Rachel safe—I had no choice but to deal.

What I *couldn't* deal with was what I saw on the far side of the mob. Morwain, fighting side by side with Rose.

"What the fuck?" I yelled, diving under a demon who was going for Rachel and slicing his belly as I slid neatly beneath him. Entrails poured out over both of us, and Rachel gagged and screamed as I pressed my switchblade into her hand. "Get back," I said. "Get back inside the pub."

Even as I said it, though, I knew she'd never make it alone.

"Come on," I said, grabbing her arm and jerking her upright. Behind us, the demon with the spilled entrails drew a last, gasping breath. Immediately, the power, the horror, the bone-deep vitriol that made up the creature's life began to swirl through me, coloring my movements, giving me confidence and, yes, strength.

"More," I said, as Deacon rushed up beside me. I

left him with Rachel, then hurried back into the fray in full attack mode, cutting the demons down like so much underbrush.

Some fought back, but most fled, with Deacon on their heels, determined not to let them leave the place. A few even bowed away, muttering about forgiveness and the *Oris Clef* and how they swore full allegiance.

A small cadre a few yards away still fought, engaging both Rose and Morwain in an intense battle. I sprinted in that direction, shouting at Rose to get the hell out of there, although I had to grudgingly admit that she was doing damned good. Balance, coordination, and she wasn't even cringing when she thrust her blade into tough demon flesh.

"Get in the pub!" I shouted. "Now!"

"A little preoccupied," she retorted.

"Get out of there," I repeated, sliding into her battle and engaging the burly demon she'd been toying with. "I don't want you getting hurt."

"You made me," she said. "You didn't want me to fight, you shouldn't have put me in a fighter's body."

I didn't point out that I hadn't exactly planned it that way. Right then, I just wanted to make her stop. But at the same time, I had to admit that it made me feel better knowing that she could hold her own.

"Lily!" Rachel called, and I turned to see Deacon battling his way to the door.

It was six against one—well, technically two, but Rachel wasn't much use—and the fury and power that was Deacon made the fight seem unfairly skewed in his direction. He thrummed and thrust and lashed and cut, his body rippling with power, the dark rolling off of him like waves to engulf his prey.

Calling for me had been an utterly superfluous act, because by the time I reached them, Deacon had laid all the attacking demons flat, and Rachel was beyond pale and breathing hard.

"Inside," Deacon said, moving for the door as I called for Morwain and Rose to hurry. Rose did, but Morwain just looked at me.

"Come on," I said. "You did good." I wasn't keen on the admission, but he had helped us. Between him and Deacon, that brought my tally of known decent demons up to two. But you had to start somewhere.

He shook his head. "Go ahead, mistress," he called, then bent over an injured demon and slammed his blade home. "Morwain will stay behind."

Couldn't argue with that. I turned back to the group, about to step into the pub. Rachel took one step, her foot almost crossing the threshold, then her body snapped tight, and I saw with horror the shaft of a crossbow arrow emerging from her back, so deep and so well placed that I was certain it must have at least nicked her heart.

She fell, her mouth open, a bubble of blood forming as she tried to speak.

I was on my knees immediately, my cry of protest so loud and anguished it ripped my throat apart. Deacon, I saw, had moved in front of us, shielding us from the attacker, and I looked up and saw where the shot had come from—the roof of the opposite building, where a man in white stood looking down at us.

"Johnson," Rose breathed.

For the first time, I didn't care. All I wanted was Rachel, and I held her hand, telling her she was going to be okay. That I'd fix it. And I was going to. Absolutely. That was one of the perks of being me, after all. I couldn't bring back the dead, but I could heal a wound.

Tears streamed down my face as I sliced my palm. And after we dragged her back inside the pub, I pulled the arrow out, terrified as I did that the damage I caused would be irreparable even for my unique skill.

I kept my hand above the wound, flexing my wrist, making fists, doing whatever it took to keep the blood flowing.

She was fading, though, and I was terrified that the injury was too severe even for me. I pressed my wrist to her lips, hoping she could just drink a few drops of my blood, but nothing seemed to be happening.

A last gasp of life racked her body, and I mourned the loss of this sister I couldn't save. This friend I'd lost, just as I'd feared I would.

But then . . .

Then she twitched. And moaned. And her tongue reached out to flick my wrist and taste my blood. My heart was tight in my chest, and I clutched her, murmuring all the stupid, useless things people say when they're sad and scared and relieved.

"He's gone," Deacon said. Through it all, he'd stood

at the window, watching that roof. "One minute he was there; the next he was gone."

"Should we be worried?" I asked.

"About Lucas Johnson? Always. But I don't think we have to worry right now."

"Whatever you say," I said, turning my attention back to Rachel. I helped her sit up, then held her tight. "You're okay now," I said. "You're going to be all right."

She turned and looked at me, her eyes glassy and her expression dim. Then she smiled, but the expression didn't last. Listlessly, she squeezed my hand. "Yes," she said. "I absolutely am."

SIXTEEN

"She'll be okay," I said, but whether I was comforting Rose or myself, I wasn't sure. We'd locked the pub up tight, then taken Rachel up to the apartment. She was in her bedroom, tucked in under the covers by two women who weren't really her sisters but had somehow become family. "She just needs sleep." I squeezed Rose's shoulder. "So do you."

She shook her head. "I'm not tired. I don't think Kiera needed to sleep."

"Just do it," I said. "I want you sharp. And I'd like you with her, too. In case she needs anything."

Rose's forehead furrowed as she glanced toward the bedroom door.

"Dammit, Rose," I said, more sharply than I'd intended. "Just go."

She scowled, but she went. And as soon as she did, I

sagged onto the couch, my thoughts racing, the dark of the kills still bubbling inside me. The sensation no longer disturbed me. On the contrary, it felt like comfort. Cold, yes, but familiar, too.

I thought of Morwain. About how he'd come when I called. About how he'd bowed when I'd given him orders. About how he'd thrust himself into the thick of battle without question or argument, simply because I said that he must.

How easy that could be, to take on the role forever. I closed my fingers around the *Oris Clef* and felt the possibility bubble and pound through me. How warm and safe that would feel, knowing that I could gather allies around me at a moment's notice.

"No," I whispered. "No, no, no."

Deacon had so far said nothing, instead standing in the dark and peering down at the street, where we had so deftly slaughtered a host of demons. Not bad for a day's work, and yet I feared . . .

I ran my finger through my hair, my thoughts trailing off, not even willing to voice in my own mind what it was that scared me. And yet, as I looked at Deacon, I knew there was no choice but to put it into words.

I stood, then took a deep breath and walked toward him. The moon, almost full, hung heavy in the sky, its light pouring in through the window and casting long shadows. The hour wasn't that late, but in October, night came early, and it felt as though it were well past midnight. Soon, it would be, and we would officially be two days away from the convergence. Less, when you considered that the final day ended at noon rather than midnight.

The time was fast approaching, and in less than forty hours, for better or for worse, we would know the way the world was going to go.

At the window, Deacon turned to watch me as I came closer. He stood perfectly still, but the wings that had become so familiar to me twitched as I approached. They'd grown and stretched during the battle, almost as if they were preening, celebrating the return to the dark.

I reached out my hand and stroked the thick, smooth skin. Deacon flinched and turned away from me.

"This is it," he said. "This is what we feared. We fight to bring order and light to the world and condemn ourselves to darkness."

He took my hand and pulled me in front of him, trapping me between his body and the window. My body cast a shadow over him, the moon's light catching him on the outside, making his body appear to glow like some sort of ethereal being. An angel. Or, at least, the way I used to believe angels appeared.

I could feel the heat from his bare chest, along with the desire. I wanted his touch—wanted nothing more than to lose myself with him, to let him claim me, to have him drive home the truth of the words he'd so often uttered. *You're mine, Lily. You're mine.*

As if understanding my need, he moved closer, his hand going to my hip. He stroked up, his thumb grazing my waist, the swell of my breast, my neck. When he reached my mouth and brought in the tip of his thumb for me to suckle, I was already limp with desire.

"Deacon," I murmured. I knew there were things to do. Things to discover. To plan and investigate. But I needed recharging. I needed humanity.

I needed, dammit, to remember why I cared so much about fighting and what exactly it was I hoped to win. I slipped my arms around his neck and moved in close, my skin humming with anticipation. I wanted to take, to demand, and the dark curls that swirled within me urged me on, begging me to grab and consume. To slam and rip and thrust and hurt—to draw the midnight black heat of this man—this demon—inside of me.

Lust swirled around us, coloring the air, our desire. His hand cupped my cheek softly, one slight, almost hesitant touch; then it was gone, his hand curling hard around my upper arm, pulling me in, claiming me with his body and his mouth. "There is a way," he said, his voice slow and overly deliberate, as if he was fighting everything within himself, including the urge to speak.

My blood pounded in my ears, my senses primed and full of desire. I didn't want to talk; I wanted *him*, and I jerked sideways, frustrated at the distraction.

He pulled me roughly back, his eyes burning into mine, then looking quick away before the *snap* that would draw me deep inside him.

"What is your nature, Lily?" he asked in a whisper as rough as sandpaper. At his back, his wings stretched and spread, filling the small corner of the room and blocking us in as effectively as if he'd built a concrete wall.

I understood. The demon inside him—it was fighting to get out. And while I knew I should help him fight back, I didn't. Because the dark within me wanted the same damn thing.

"At heart, Lily, are you good or are you bad?"

My head snapped up in surprise, because that was a question to which I really no longer knew the answer.

He tilted his head, looking at me, his eyes cunning and devious, yet inviting. As if everything would be all right if I simply trusted him.

Faith, Lily.

Slowly, his hand reached out, and he stroked my jaw, the touch sending electric tingles racing through me. The finger traced down, finding the chain of the *Oris Clef,* and he brushed the tip of the digit along the woven metal, then pressed his palm over the gemstone and the ornate cage that held it.

"I can make a Heaven of Hell," he said, so softly I had to strain to hear him. *"What matter where, if I still be the same?* Milton was right, Lily. You would be the same. At your heart, at your core. Bring them. Lead them. You have the key. It's destiny, Lily, and you're the one who can save us all."

I shook my head, not quite able to process what he was saying. This was *Deacon.* A demon, yes, but my anchor, and the words he spoke . . . He couldn't mean them. Could he?

"Lily, you know it's true. You feel it. I know, because I feel it, too."

I drew in a breath and realized as I did so that I was

trembling, my head moving slowly back and forth, the faith I'd had in Deacon faltering, shaking the entire foundation of what I'd built. But at the same time . . .

At the same time I had to wonder if he was right. If maybe this was my destiny. Reign, and change the future. Reign, and make a heaven of a world that would change in less than two days.

It was tempting. To rule with Deacon at my side. To know that I was in charge. That I could keep those I loved close to me.

"I don't know," I whispered, my head a muddle, the darkness within me curling slowly, sensuously. Filling and warming me, and it felt nice. Good. It felt *safe*. "I don't know what to do."

"Then let me help you."

"You really want me to rule?" I looked up at him and felt tears well in my eyes. "What about finding the blade? Finding redemption?"

He turned away, his expression hard. "There is no redemption. Not for me. But I always said that we would see this through together." He turned back, and I saw the determination in his expression, along with the lust. Only not for me—for power. "Reign, and you can keep them safe. Rachel. Rose. Do this, Lily, and—"

Faith, Lily . . .

But this *wasn't* Deacon. This wasn't the Deacon I desired. The Deacon I could cling to. This was someone else. This was the Deacon who'd deserved the fires of hell. The Deacon who scared me, and I feared that the Deacon I wanted—the Deacon I loved—had been lost. Buried beneath the force of this man who'd burst free when the demon had come out.

Faith, Lily . . .

But how could I rely on faith when the one thing I'd clung to rose wrongfully in front of me. When the small kernel of faith I'd placed in the man had been shattered?

"Lily," he whispered. "You know I'm right."

"No." I shoved him, hard, but not hard enough to move him. He stood before me like stone, and I could do nothing but beat my fists uselessly against his chest, wanting *my* Deacon back, and cursing him for not fighting harder. For not battling back the darkness that was rising in him.

Because he had to fight it back. If he didn't—if he couldn't—then the faith I'd managed to dredge up, despite this totally fucked-up world, had been wholly and utterly misplaced.

"No," I repeated, battling down my own temptation, the curls of darkness that longed to take what Deacon said and make it my own. *"No."*

I stepped closer, pressing against him. "Fight, dammit. This isn't you."

He tilted his head to look down at me, his eyes as black as midnight. "It's me, Lily."

I trembled, fearing that he was right. But if so, that meant that I'd lost the Deacon I knew. The Deacon I loved.

"Dammit, Deacon—" I grabbed his head and pulled it down to me, kissing him hard. Wanting to get through to him and not knowing how. I pulled away, fast and quick, then met his eyes. And then, before I could talk myself out of it, I reached out and slapped him hard across the cheek.

He jerked back, releasing a breath so low it sounded like a hiss. His eyes flared, and I tensed, ready for a fight—*wanting* the fight. But it didn't come. Instead, he stood there, wary, and I saw awareness in those eyes. I saw the fight, hiding there, ready to burst free. But it wasn't popping, and so I reached out and slapped him again.

"Fight, dammit! That's what you are! You're a fighter. So *fight*, already." I felt the wetness on my cheeks and knew that I was crying, and when he reached out to grab my wrist as I lashed out yet again, I choked out a wet, tearful sob.

He jerked me roughly to him. "You play a dangerous game, Lily."

"Not a game," I said. "You've survived this shit once already. You can do it. Come back to me." And with that, I pressed close once again and captured his mouth in mine. The kiss was hard, violent, yet filled with a desperate intensity. *You're mine,* I wanted to say. *You're mine, dammit. Come back to me.*

He moaned, the sound so full of soft desire I wanted to cry again. And then he pushed me back, so roughly I slammed against the window ledge. He backed up, his hands to his head, his body hunched over as the battle raged within him.

He lashed out, breaking the coffee table, overturning

the couch, slamming his hand through the wall. His body was a war zone, and I could see his flesh moving as the demon within fought for control.

The battle was bitter and long and utterly destructive, and I stood helplessly, able only to watch and to hope.

And then I saw him go still. Saw him tilt his head back and howl, his arms thrust out at his sides. He stayed like that, the echo of his voice reverberating off the walls, and when the room was in silence again, he looked at me, his face flush with victory, his wings now gone.

He'd won.

He'd beaten back the demons, and a swell of both relief and hope coursed through me. Relief that he was back, and hope that—when such a bitter battle faced me—I could find in me the same strength that Deacon found within himself.

He held out his hand to me, and I came, closing my hand over his as he drew me in closer. I stroked his body, finding his back perfectly smooth, the wings having been completely reabsorbed, subjugated to the force of Deacon's will.

"You're back," I whispered, falling into his arms.

"I am," he said, but what I heard was, "Thank you."

A sharp sound on the far side of the room had us pulling apart quickly, and I whipped around to see Rose standing there, her expression wary as she eyed the war zone that the room had become. "I—I heard—"

"It's okay," I said. "We're fine."

She shook her head. "No, not you." She frowned at the mess as if considering amending that statement. "I heard sirens. Outside, you know? And I decided to turn on the television in the bedroom, and—" Her voice broke, and I rushed toward her.

"Rose?"

She pointed to the television and I turned it on. Total coverage of disasters around the world. Earthquakes, fires, dormant volcanoes suddenly spewing forth molten rock from the bowels of the earth. Some of the stations had scientific commentators trying to expound a science-based reason for all of this. Others had brought on religious gurus, who either professed gloom and doom or concentrated on getting the audience to repent.

I knew the real explanation, of course. Penemue. Kokbiel. And the horrific tug of the convergence coming closer and closer.

Not our usual television-watching fare, but considering Rose already knew all that was happening, I wasn't entirely sure what the problem was.

"Wait," she said, grabbing the remote and switching to a local news channel. "See?"

I saw—and my mouth went dry.

Riots at St. Jerome's. Fifteen dead, including responding police officers. Forty-seven injured. And in the background, the battle raged on, and damned if I didn't recognize some of the faces brandishing weapons and cutting down humans. Damned if I hadn't served them pints and let them sit in my pub.

"That's where he lives, right? That priest you talked to?"

I nodded, my eyes glued to the television. "But the demons can't go there," I said, glancing quickly at Deacon.

He frowned. "The convergence. As it gets closer, things break down, and even holy places become the most desperate of battlefields. Especially holy places."

And wasn't that special?

"Is that—?" Rose's finger was extended toward the screen, and I saw the monsignor amidst a crush of demons, his lips moving in silent prayer.

"Oh, no," I whispered. I wanted to go to him, to help him, but I didn't know if I should. My battle was coming—could I risk the world for the sake of one man?

"Him," Deacon said. "The demon right there." He tapped the screen, indicating a demon with white hair standing just behind the one who held the priest. "He's a Caller."

I said a silent thank-you, because since we didn't have the knife, we still needed the Caller. Get the Caller, save the priest. It was practically a two-for-one special.

"I have to go." I was halfway to the door before the words were out of my mouth.

"Not alone," Deacon said, immediately at my side.

I looked at him, then at the television screen. Then I shook my head. "It's too soon," I said. "And you're too exhausted from the fight."

"The hell I am."

But I knew I was right. "Stay," I said. "I need you to protect Rachel, anyway. I have a feeling that once she decided to mess with the demons, the protections on this place started melting away. The demons may not realize it yet, but—"

"They will," he said. "And yeah, I think you're right."

"You mean we're not safe here anymore?" Rose asked.

I shook my head. "I don't think anywhere is safe anymore."

She licked her lips, looking worried, as I turned back to Deacon. "Please," I said. "Don't fight me on this. I need you here watching Rachel. And I don't want you—"

I couldn't finish, my words choking off instead.

"I don't want you going alone," he said.

I looked at Rose. I didn't want to admit she had the fight in her—didn't want to acknowledge that she was truly part of this world. But the time for wishful thinking was over. From there on out, it was all about action.

"Don't worry," I said to Deacon as I held out a hand to Rose. "I won't be."

SEVENTEEN

Thwack!

The demon caught me dead across the jaw, and I lashed back, pissed off and ready for the kill.

Rose got there first, thrusting her blade deep into my attacker's chest. It collapsed into a pile of goo, and she shot me a look of triumph despite the fact that we were hardly done yet. Hell, we'd barely even started.

"Thanks," I said, because it wasn't the time to mourn the loss of the little sister I remembered or to remind her to be careful. We were in the thick of it, and the only truly useful thing to do was fight.

Which we were doing. Hard and fast and furious.

We'd arrived at the church in record speed, having taken the Tiger, which I'd brought back to the pub after we'd scoured Alice's apartment. I'd feared that we'd have to do some song-and-dance routine to get past the police and emergency services responders, but we hadn't, most likely because they were all dead, and I was terrified that the monsignor was as well.

That terror spurred me on, pushing us into the fray, killing and fighting and battling demon after demon as they surged backward, gathering their forces in the bowels of the building.

I'd called for Morwain when we'd arrived, and at first, he'd battled right beside us, his own blade out, his fingers elongated with razor-sharp talons. But now, as I watched in horror, he bent over the corpse of a teenage boy, peeled a strip of flesh, and ate it.

I turned away, gagging, my mind swimming with what he was, this creature that so willingly did my bidding.

"Mistress," he said, bowing low, his mouth bloody.

"The demons," I said, forcing my voice steady and aiming my gaze in the direction the throng had traveled. "Cut them down, cut through them, but don't stop until you find the monsignor." I cast a gaze at the body on the floor. "Don't stop for anything."

"Yes, mistress," he said, then disappeared into the dark. I watched him go, imagining him swallowed up by the belly of the beast. Imagining that we all were. I drew in a shaky breath and pressed my hand against Rose's shoulder. I told myself not to second-guess my decision to bring her, but I couldn't help it. I knew it was a mistake. I only hoped that my mistake wouldn't get my sister killed.

"Do you think he's . . ." Rose asked, unable to give voice to the real question.

"I don't know," I admitted. "I hope not, but we're not here just for him."

"The Caller," she said.

"Come on," I said to Rose, then started stalking through the wreckage, following the path Morwain had taken. "Careful," I added. "And alert."

"I know," she said, but there was no verbal eye roll, no hint of sarcasm. She was doing this right, and a tiny weight lifted from me. Maybe she'd get through unscathed.

Maybe we both would.

We found Morwain in the little garden area where I'd spoken with the priest. Although, to be perfectly accurate, we found him on the path, and on the flower bed, and in the trees.

"Oh God," Rose said, clutching her stomach as she stepped back from the bloody remains of the demon that had pledged service to me.

"Didn't much like the bloody bugger," a broad-chested demon said, stepping forward from a throng of dark, smelly demons of both the humanoid and the monstrous variety. He wore tattered pants, as if he'd been pumped up with the dark so much that the seams had burst. His chest was bare and covered with ancient symbols. His face was red and oozing, as though someone had pressed his head into a red-hot iron skillet. A thick dribble of puss oozed down his cheek before a lizardlike tongue whipped out and flicked it away. "Guess he was confused about where his allegiance should be placed."

"He wasn't confused. His allegiance lay with this." I took a bold step forward, holding up the *Oris Clef.* "Pay it respect," I said. "Pay *me* respect, or in two short days you're going to find yourselves very, very miserable." To my credit, my voice didn't waver, and I kept my head held high. Behind the leader, a few beasties shifted, as if, maybe, they were questioning the wisdom of pissing me off. One of them, I saw with glee, was the Caller.

I raised my voice. "Go now, and I'll forget I ever saw you. Stay," I added, lowering my voice to a growl, "and you'll soon learn how painful my displeasure can be."

At first I feared that I'd gone too far. Then a cluster of demons broke off the pack, skulking out the back and avoiding the furious glares of the leader in front. I forced myself not to cheer, and instead stood tall and quiet, as if I'd expected nothing less.

"Fool," I said. "You should have gone with your little friends."

"And you," he said, with a growl, "should remember that you are neither as clever nor as strong as we who live in the dark." He stepped aside, revealing the demon behind him, the monsignor trapped in his arms, ready to be pulled apart limb by limb. "You can still save him, you know. All you have to do is give me that which you wear around your neck."

"No." I spoke firmly, trying to hide the horror in my voice. But I knew it came through anyway. I knew because of the way the demon smiled at me with smug

satisfaction. He'd won a round, he knew. And I was certain that he expected he'd win another.

Fuck.

The leader twisted his neck to look at the demons behind him, his hideous mouth pulling into a delighted smile. "You see? Did I not tell you she would come? The key, little bitch. Give us the *Oris Clef*, and this pitiful human can live."

I took a step forward, not certain what I planned to do, but knowing I had to do something. I couldn't stand there and watch them kill a priest.

Rose's hand on my arm pulled me back. "You can't give it to him," she said. "After everything Deacon did to hide it—after everything you did to keep it away from Penemue—God, Lily, you can't just turn it over now." She turned to look at the monsignor, and I saw the tears trickle down her cheeks. "It's war, Lily, and the demons can't win. You know what they're like. You know what they'll do."

I could hear it in her voice. The terror. The memories. Everything she'd suffered at Lucas Johnson's hands coming right back to haunt her.

There was no way I was giving up the *Oris Clef*, but neither was I giving up that innocent man without a fight. "We fight," I said, and even before the words were out of my mouth, my knife was out of my hand, spinning blade over hilt toward the demon that held the priest. It landed true, right in the bastard's eye, and as the monsignor fell to the floor, the demon's body dissolved into a thick, viscous oil that dripped down onto him, covering his arms and legs until it finally disappeared into the floor, a greasy stain the only evidence his captor had once been there.

I'd brought a second blade, too, and I sent it flying as well, but that time, I'd lost the element of surprise. As the throng rushed forward toward Rose and me, the lead demon leaped sideways, even as the Caller raced toward the fallen priest. I whirled toward him, yanking the sword from the scabbard at my back, and shouted for him to stop.

He did, but only once he had the priest in front of him.

I froze, eyeing the knife he held at the old man's throat.

"Do not fear," the priest said, and when he looked at me, it was Gabriel's face I saw. "My faith will keep me strong."

I stumbled backward, then willed myself to stay in the game, not to react to the hallucinations, if that even was what they were.

"Shall I do it?" the Caller said. "Shall I bleed him?"

I hesitated, because Rose slid up beside me and pressed a blade into my hand. I recognized it as my own, and I held it tight. More than that, I saw opportunity.

I could save the monsignor. I was certain of it. I could save him by killing the Caller, who towered at least a head taller than the priest. I was sure of my aim, certain of my target.

I could do this.

And if I did, the Caller demon would die.

If I didn't, the priest would.

Did I sacrifice the priest for the slim chance of finding the blade?

Or did I kill the Caller and have faith that somehow it would all turn out okay?

So far, faith and I weren't the best buddies, but I was trying. And when I looked in the old man's eyes, I knew I had to try once again.

I clutched my knife, took a breath, and sent the blade flying.

It got the Caller dead in the eye, just as I knew it would.

But it didn't matter.

In the split second it had taken for me to contemplate my faith, the Caller had taken his own knife and slit the monsignor's throat.

I'd lost them both, Caller and priest.

I'd gambled on faith, and I'd lost.

So far, I thought, that had been the story of my life.

I saw the body fall, heard Rose's frustrated cry, and caught the scent of fresh blood on the air. Within me, the newly dead demons writhed and preened, gaining satisfaction from the massacre and screaming for another kill—demon, human, they didn't care.

I did, though. *I cared.*

I grabbed Rose by the arm and dragged her back toward the door.

"The priest!" Rose called. "Can't you—"

"He's dead," I said flatly. I could heal, but I couldn't

resurrect. I'd lost him, and now I had the weight of another priest's death on my shoulder, counterbalanced by the weight of the whole damn world.

Having lost their hostages and their leader, the demons were a disorganized mob, and though I wouldn't say they were happy to let us go, the battle to get back out on the street was quick and dirty, and ended with Rose and I both increasing our dead demon head count.

All good and well, except once we were free and standing outside in the light of the almost-full moon, I could see a gang of demons marching toward us, the blades they held in their hands glinting in the soft glow, their faces—or what could reasonably be called faces—twisting with malicious purpose.

"Forget fighting," I said. "Just run." We did, only to find the way to the Tiger blocked. "Fuck it," I said, then smashed in the window of a nearby car. "In!"

"Hurry!" Rose said, bouncing on the passenger seat as demons reached through the hole in the window, trying to drag us back out.

This model was harder to get started, but I finally got the engine going, and I gunned it, aiming that puppy not away from the demons but toward them. And I didn't take my foot off the accelerator for an instant.

The sickening sound of flesh torn apart by metal echoed around us, accompanied by the slightly squishy sound of bloody body parts splattered on the hood and windshield.

I pressed on, flicking the wipers on to see better, and

trying to ignore the fact that none of this seemed to faze Rose, who took my Demon Derby approach to driving in stride.

By the time we got back to the pub, I was frustrated and pissed, the burden of the monsignor's death weighing on me all the more because I'd lost the Caller demon, too, and time was running out, moonrise on the day of the convergence fast approaching.

Fuck.

I was moving to the bar to pull myself a Guinness when Deacon and Rachel came down. "Any demon activity while I was gone?" I asked, looking at each of them in turn.

"I just woke up," Rachel said, ignoring the way Rose scooted over to make room for her in a nearby booth and instead settling onto a stool at the bar. "One for me, too."

Rachel was more of a wine sipper than beer guzzler, but I wasn't going to deny her a fast slug of a thick brew, and I passed her a pint, then took a long draw of my own before pulling another for Deacon.

"Well?" I asked.

He looked at me, his eyes seeing more than I wanted. "What happened?"

"What do you think happened?" I spat, slamming the pint down and sloshing beer everywhere. *"Dammit."* I got a towel and started mopping furiously, determined not to cry.

Damn.

I turned away, feeling their eyes on me. I kept my

back pressed against the oak, my face turned toward the tower of bottles. I could see them, like modern art, reflected in the bottles and the bar mirror. Rachel and Deacon nearby, Rose curled up back in a booth. Rose looked a little shell-shocked, the way I felt. Deacon looked firm, resolute. Like a soldier, and I took some comfort in that.

And Rachel . . .

Rachel just looked like she wished this whole thing were over.

Well, I thought, *don't we all?*

"He had his faith to the end," Deacon said. "And we will find the key even without the Caller."

"How?" I said, rounding on him. "How are we supposed to do that?"

"I don't know."

That was all he said. Just, "I don't know." But I heard so much more in those two little words. I heard compassion and understanding. I heard the reflection of everything he'd lost in his time upon this earth. Of everything he wanted to gain.

And I heard the promise that he would stand beside me as I fought my way through the pain. As we figured this out together.

Maybe I was reading too much into those two little words, but as I looked at his face—at the warmth in his eyes—I didn't think so.

And I damn sure hoped I wasn't wrong.

EIGHTEEN

Time was ticking down fast, and without the Caller demon, I was beginning to fear we were completely screwed, and I was kicking myself for acting so rashly and not figuring out a way to save the priest and catch the demon. Or maybe I should have just sacrificed the monsignor. I didn't know.

For that matter, all I did know was that the only thing in the whole world I needed was to figure out where Alice's mom had hidden the dagger, and as to that I was having absolutely no luck despite the fact that we all spent hours searching the apartment and the bar for any talisman that Alice's mom might have used to hide the key and Egan might have then taken and hidden himself.

Nothing.

"The book," I said as late afternoon rolled in. "It has to be. It's the only thing that makes sense."

"It didn't work," Deacon said. "Worse, you were almost destroyed."

I had to admit that was definitely a downside. "But what else can it be? Unless the portal's hidden in one of Alice's kitchen knives."

"Or a letter opener," Rose added, in a distinctly unhelpful comment.

"I have to try again," I said.

Rachel crossed her arms over her chest and frowned. "I don't know . . ."

"Right now, I'm the one calling the shots," I said. "And I am trying again." I pointed to Rose. "Go get the book."

To her credit, she didn't argue, merely trotted upstairs, then returned with the battered tome. She set it on the bar, and we all peered at it, keeping our distance as if the thing could bite.

Deacon stepped up beside me and took my hand, prepared to be my anchor despite his objections to the experiment.

"Here goes nothing," I said. I opened the book back up to the inscription, sliced my palm, pressed, and waited for the jolt.

It didn't come.

"What's happening?" Rachel asked.

"Nothing," I admitted, opening my eyes. "Not a thing."

"No rumble? No yank on your gut?" Rose asked.

"I said nothing," I snapped, irritated more by the failure than by her questions. I reined in the urge to toss the book across the room. Instead, I ripped my hand free from Deacon and stalked to the back. I opened the walk-in freezer, found the ice cream, and proceeded to dig it out with an industrial-size spoon.

When all else fails, sometimes you have to fall back on the old standbys.

Rose came in to the freezer with me, made a face, then took the ice cream from my hands. I protested—I really needed that chocolate—then realized she was only leading me out of the chill. We parked ourselves at the small table where Caleb the cook sat to get off his feet during his shift. I wasn't in the mood to get up and search for another spoon, so I shared the one I had with Rose.

"We used to do this at home," she said.

"I remember."

"Do you think it'll ever be like that again?"

There was hope in her voice, and I hated the thought of killing it. So I reached for her hand and squeezed. "Sure."

Her smile was sad. "Liar."

"Losing faith already?" It wouldn't surprise me. Goodness knew *my* belief that I would find the missing key was fading fast.

"No," she said, her voice so sincere it made my heart swell. "But even after we stop it, the world's never going to be the same, right? I mean, people have *seen*."

I nodded, wondering if she was right. They'd seen, yes, but had they understood? People, I knew, had an amazing capacity for rationalizing everything, and I wouldn't put it past them to rationalize the end of the world, too.

"What's going to happen?" Rose asked, picking at her cuticles instead of looking at me. "If you can't find the lost key, I mean?"

I grimaced. Because wasn't that the question of the hour? "Don't worry," I said. "I will."

It wasn't a promise I could be sure of keeping, but it was one I meant with all my heart.

I took a final bite of ice cream and headed back into the pub to see if Deacon had come up with any brilliant ideas, because without that damn missing key, I was right back where we started, with me staring into that rock and edging up against that proverbial hard place.

In the front of the pub, Deacon was stalking across the floor, his body tense, his gaze darting out the window at the coming dawn. There was a tension about him that made me nervous, and I moved toward him, wary, my gaze on his back in case any wings decided to sprout.

"Deacon?"

He paused in his pacing, then turned to me, moving slowly, as if he had to focus on every step. A man trying hard to stay connected to this reality.

"Can you feel it?" he asked. "The pull. Like a rubber band tight around your middle."

"I—"

"And the sound. Like swarming bees." He tilted his head to the side, his eyes narrowing. "They're readying." He looked at me. "They're coming."

"I know," I said, wary. I'd been feeling it myself, that subtle tug. And along with it, the *Oris Clef* had been calling out to me more and more, teasing and tempting me. I was fighting it, yes, but it was getting harder.

It was getting harder for Deacon, too.

"I won't join them. I won't turn again." He craned his neck, looking at his back. "I swear to you now, Lily, that I will not fail in this fight. I will not turn again."

I moved to him, felt his arms go tight around me. "I know. That's not who you are. Not anymore."

He pulled back, then hooked his finger under my chin. "And you?"

I stepped away, ashamed, my fingers going to the *Oris Clef*, hanging around my neck. I could feel its power in my hand. Like Deacon, it was attuned to the coming convergence, and it thrummed with energy, warming my hand and fueling thoughts that I had no business thinking. I knew I shouldn't even open myself to the temptation. But I couldn't deny that the temptation was there.

"I'm running out of options," was all I said, and he nodded, his breath releasing on a sigh.

I was also running out of time. I hadn't seen Penemue or Kokbiel or Gabriel, but I knew that wasn't because they were being polite and waiting for engraved invitations. No, they were gathering strength. Waiting until closer to the convergence. Planning to swoop in and take either the key or me, then use it as the portal peeled open.

Soon. Very soon.

We stood there a moment, Deacon and I, looking out onto the night. The street was gray, covered in a thin ash from fires that raged throughout the town. The street was cracked, the aftereffects of a series of tiny earthquakes. No teenagers walked the streets; no cars purred down the road. The world, it seemed, was dying. Humanity might not understand why, but it knew it was ill. Knew that the final death throes were upon it.

Rachel came up softly behind us. "Do we have a plan? Do you two have any idea about the missing key? Any idea at all where it might be?"

I shook my head, frustrated to have to admit that we did not.

She frowned, then took my arm and tugged me aside. Deacon didn't notice; he was back to staring out the window, the fight within him already having begun.

"Rachel? What is it?"

Her brow furrowed as her lips pressed together. She glanced over her shoulder to where Rose was now tossing her knife at the dartboard, hitting bull's-eye after bull's-eye.

"Nothing," she said, then turned away.

I pulled her back. "Wait. Hang on. You pulled me aside, remember? It's not nothing." I saw the battle play out across her face, the hard-fought question of should she, or should she not tell me whatever it was that was on her mind.

"It's just that—it's just that I know you."

"I—okay." I had no idea what I was supposed to say,

or for that matter if I needed to say anything at all. "Um, so?"

She ran her fingers through her hair, tousling it in a way which suggested she was even more disturbed than she was letting on. Rachel, I'd learned, was nothing if not put together. "I just mean that even though it hasn't been that long, I really feel like I know you. And it's not just an illusion—I'm not having fantasies that you're really Alice, or that some part of her lives on inside you. I know you." Her brow furrowed. "Your heart, I mean."

"This is all really nice," I said. "And I appreciate the pep talk. But I'm on the clock here, and I should probably go see what Deacon's doing, because if he doesn't come through with a Caller demon, I—"

"Use the key," she said. "*Do it*. Use the *Oris Clef*."

I gaped at her. "You can't be serious."

"Hell, yes, I am," she said, leaning forward and eyeing me earnestly. "Don't you see? It's like I said before—black magic's only black if you use it that way. But you're *good*. You step up and take the throne, and you'll have an opportunity no one has ever had before. You'll have the chance to take something dark and make it light. To take evil and turn it around until you don't even recognize it anymore. You can eradicate it, Lily. Don't you see? You have the chance to have a legacy here. And, honestly, I think it's what you were meant to do. I think it's why you're here."

"I don't know," I said, though I had to admit there was some sense to what she said. After all, I'd been fighting the demonic essence inside of me for a while. I'd gotten it down. Figured it out. More or less, anyway.

Surely it wouldn't be harder when I was the queen. Hell, it might even be easier. How many queens personally executed the bad guys?

I'd be the Gentle Demon Queen. Lily the Great, who goes down in history as the woman who ushered in a new era. Who merged the realms of dark and light.

The woman who tamed the demons.

And how much easier would that be than the alternative? An eternity so vile I couldn't even wrap my head about it. So horrible that the mere thought of it brought the stench of death back to me, making me gag and whimper merely from the possibility. "I don't know," I said. But I was tempted—hell, I'd been tempted when Deacon had suggested it, too. And I could tell by Rachel's expression that she knew that I was.

"You just think about it, okay? Because I can't see you being evil."

I frowned. Because I could see it. Hell, I'd looked into the future through Gabriel's eyes, and I'd seen it bright and clear, me standing there, ushering the demons over to this world.

"I'll keep an open mind," I finally said, forcing myself not to think about the rest of it. About how Deacon had wanted that role for me so desperately when he was in his demonic form and wanted me to steer far away now that he was himself again. Those were anomalies that weighed against Rachel's suggestion, even though, at the moment, I was rather liking Rachel's idea. Or, at least, I was liking the idea of surviving.

I tilted my head, something curious occurring to me. "When did I tell you about the *Oris Clef*?"

"Oh," she said, her eyes shifting from left to right, then finally landing on Rose. "Don't say anything to her, okay? I don't want to get her in trouble."

"Rose told you?" Anger fluttered within me. She'd stood right there when I'd deliberately not told Rachel, then she went and blabbed anyway?

"She's a kid," Rachel said. "And she's scared for you."

I brushed it away, because Rachel was right, of course. "I'm scared for me, too," I said. "I'm scared for all of us. And I'm horribly afraid that I'm missing something huge. Something that I'm not seeing or . . ." I trailed off with a shrug. "I don't know. My brain is fried."

"So what's bothering you?" She laughed, the sound a little hollow. "Besides the obvious, I mean."

"Lucas Johnson, for one thing. He was so hot to get this thing," I said, pointing to the *Oris Clef* at my neck. "And now he's just disappeared."

"But you knocked him out of Rose's body."

"He has a new one, though. I saw him, too. When you were attacked. He was standing on a rooftop, watching, like he had front-row seats to a basketball game or something."

"You're sure it was him?"

"I'm sure."

"Then you're probably right. He's probably up to something."

Despite the fact that I did not want to have to mess with Johnson again, my shoulders sagged with relief that she agreed with me. "Yes," I said eagerly. "It's not like him to hang back, especially when everything is coming to a head so soon." Even if I did want to use the *Oris Clef*—and tempting though it might be, I wasn't saying I did—I had to figure that Johnson was waiting somewhere, all poised and ready to yank the thing away from me.

So why hadn't he tried yet? I didn't get it. And I don't like things that I didn't get.

I reached up to hold the *Oris Clef*, so warm in my hand. Like Deacon, it could feel the coming of the convergence, and I wished it could show me the future. The true future.

"I don't think I could control it," I said to Rachel.

"Sweetie, you're stronger than you think."

I drew in a breath, then shifted so I could look back at Rose. I'd been the big sister for so long, but I didn't want to be anymore. I wanted someone to tell me what to do for once, and I turned back to Rachel, then reached for her. I took her hands, then looked at her, my mouth open to tell her please just help me figure it out.

I never got the question out. Instead, I snapped into her. I heard her gasp, felt her pull away, but not before I got a glimpse of something dark. Something hidden.

"Dammit, Lily! You're not supposed to get in people's heads!"

"I'm sorry," I said. "I swear it was an accident." But even as I spoke, I wished that I'd found the time to learn to be stealthy like Madame Parrish had suggested. As it was, I had only that one image, and in truth, it worried me. Because Rachel had once been a disciple of the dark, just like her uncle Egan. She'd given it all up, and I believed her. But that didn't mean she couldn't relapsc.

These were dark times after all, and the pull of the dark was powerful. Rachel might want a clean break, but that didn't mean she would get one. The dark could suck you in, after all.

I understood that better than anyone.

NINETEEN

I was near the front of the pub, ostensibly checking the locks, but really trying to think about anything but what was happening. Anything but the choices I had to make.

"They're out there," I said, as Deacon approached. "Can you see them?"

"I can smell them," he said, peering out the curtain beside me. "They'll come in, soon. They want what you have, and they can't wait much longer. Either that, or they want to rip you apart so that you can't stop what's coming."

I snorted. "I don't know if I *can* stop it anyway." I swallowed. "I mean, I know I *can*. I just don't know if I—"

He pressed a finger to my lips. "We'll find it."

I grimaced. Unless he had some magic spell I was unaware of tucked up his sleeve, I was thinking that wasn't damn likely. The night had passed without attacks from the demons—and that was good—but it had also passed without us finding Margaret's dagger. And that was bad.

Also on the bad side, the demons appeared to be shifting their approach. They'd left us alone for the night, but on this last day we were no longer going to be so lucky. Time kept rushing forward, and with it, the end of the world.

"Are you ready to fight?" he asked, nodding toward the door. I wasn't. I was tired of fighting. Terrified, too, that if I killed any more demons, I would no longer have the strength—no, the *desire*—to fight the allure of the talisman around my neck. An allure that was getting stronger with each passing minute.

I wanted to shield myself. From the call of the dark. From the demons. From every damn thing, but I didn't know how. It wasn't like I could put a little force field around myself and—

Oh.

"Protections," I said triumphantly. No help for the battle I'd have to fight at the bridge, but at least we'd continue to be safe inside the pub.

"Broken," he countered. "We already talked about that."

"We need new ones," I said, then signaled for Rachel to come over. "They're going to come in," I said without preamble. "Can you do a protection spell? Can you replace the ones that were broken?"

She seemed to go a little pale. "I—I'm not sure. Over this whole place?"

"It doesn't have to last forever," I said. "Just a few hours. I know you don't want to—I know I'm making you do something you gave up—but you said it yourself, right? It's only black magic if you use it for the dark."

She licked her lips. "Just a few hours?"

I glanced at Deacon. For better or for worse, we needed to be out of here and on the bridge soon. So yeah, this was a temporary gig. "Absolutely," I said.

I felt a little guilty that she looked so trapped, but not enough to ask her not to at least try. Maybe it wouldn't work, but we needed something to go right for us, and we wouldn't know unless she tried. After a moment, she nodded. "All right. But this is a solitary spell. Don't disturb me. I'll let you know when the building is secure."

I glanced at Deacon and noticed the way his head was cocked, as if he was listening for something. I knew what, because I was listening, too. And I heard them as well. "Fine," I told Rachel. "But hurry."

As she went off to gather supplies, I turned to Deacon. "They're going to completely surround the place. Are we going to be able to get out when we need to?"

"Portal," he said, and I blanched.

"But the time thing. If we miss the convergence—"

"We won't. Rachel and Rose stay here, safe in the protection spell. Between the two of them, they can anchor us."

"You're sure?"

His eyes darted to Rachel. "If she's strong enough to do a protection spell with the convergence this close, she's strong enough to be an anchor. And Rose has her own strength."

That she had, and knowing that she would be safe within the pub would help me fight, too. And I was going to have to fight—I knew that. Penemue or Kokbiel—or both—would be there trying to get the *Oris Clef*.

And as for me?

Hopefully, I'd be trying to use a dagger that Margaret had hidden so that her daughter could save the world. But I had my doubts.

Without thinking, I closed my hand around the *Oris Clef*, feeling its call, its promise. Maybe Rachel was right. After all, the black arts were only black if you used them that way. If I used my position for the good of humanity rather than its degradation . . .

I closed my eyes, picturing the transition as I'd seen it in Gabriel's mind. The portal opening. The demons barreling toward us through the vortex that would open to allow passage between the worlds. And me standing at the threshold, my knife tight in my hand as I slice my palm, as I grasp the *Oris Clef* with my bloodied hand and recite the words that would make me queen.

My bloodied hand . . .

The image swirled in my head, and when I opened my eyes, I saw Deacon watching me warily. "What?" he asked.

"My blood," I whispered. "It's always been about my blood." I looked wildly around for the book I thought we'd left on the bar. "Where is it? Where's the book?"

From near the dartboard, Rose glanced over. "I took it back upstairs."

"Right." I squeezed Deacon's hand. "Stay with them. Make sure the protections work."

"What are you—"

But I was gone, racing toward the back, shouting at Rachel to finish the protections and stay there with Deacon.

"Wait!" she called, running after me.

"Rachel!" I paused at the bottom of the stairs. "Bit of a time crunch here . . ."

"What's going on?"

"I think I know where the missing key is. Just keep it up, okay? We need to have this place safe again."

"What? Where?"

"Protections!" I shouted over my shoulder as I tromped up the stairs, my fingers and all other appendages crossed tightly. Mentally crossed, at any rate.

I burst into the apartment and found the book on the kitchen table. *Thank goodness*. I just prayed that I was right.

The worn image of a dagger on the cover was barely visible, but to me, it was about the most beautiful thing ever. "Please," I whispered. "Please be right."

I drew in a breath, then sliced my hand. I held it over the book and let my blood drip on the image of the dagger. At first, I thought nothing would happen. Then the image started to fill out, the lines becoming solid, then the picture taking on form, bubbling up from the cover of the book.

"The key . . ."

Rachel's awed voice from the doorway made me jump, and I turned to frown at her. "Dammit, Rachel! I told you to stay downstairs."

"I know," she said. "But my mother hid the dagger for my sister. I should be here."

"Downstairs?"

"All taken care of," she said. She took a step closer, her eyes wide with wonder, her finger reaching out as if to stroke the blade.

"Lily!" Rose's anguished cry echoed up from downstairs.

"Shit!" I said, immediately pushing past Rachel, who cried for me to hurry, then gave me a sharp and slightly painful shove in the direction of the door.

But I didn't make it.

There was something wrong. Something very wrong—and very familiar.

Paralytic.

I'd been hit with it before, by Deacon, actually, back when he thought we were on opposites sides. Now, apparently, Rachel had gotten me.

"What?" I said, but that was all I got out before my mouth failed me, and I dropped to the floor, trying to fight the drug. Trying to just keep breathing.

Rachel bent over in front of me and took the knife.

"Stupid girl," she said, in a voice not Rachel's but which I recognized nonetheless—*Lucas Johnson.* "I could wait—I could risk—you having the *Oris Clef.* I could even encourage it. Tempt you. Tease you. Keep you from searching for the missing key. Keep you from thinking like a damned foolish martyr. So long as the portal opens there's a chance for us. The hordes cross, and we are in a new world order.

"Even if I failed at the bridge and you claimed the throne, you'd never be strong enough to keep it. How could you be when everything you are, everything you ever will be comes from me? I'm stronger because I made you. Planned you. I fucking *controlled* you. And you never even had a clue."

Disgust and self-loathing welled within me, but there was nothing I could do. Nothing except lie there and wait for him to cut me to pieces.

"And after my coup—after I cut you up and put the bits of your body in little boxes hidden all over the earth—the world will be remade in my image and the image of him that I serve, Kokbiel, the most powerful." He smiled. "Lucky me that I don't have to wait on that part now." He held up the knife. "A key that will lock the gates? Sorry, daughter-dear, but I can't let you use this. But the blade seems sharp enough." He bent close to me. "Perhaps we'll get some use out of it before I destroy it for good."

He squatted beside me, and I tried desperately not to let the terror I felt show in my eyes. This was it—the thing I had feared most of all since the moment I'd learned I was immortal. That I would be alive and non-functional. Alive, yet boxed up. Spread apart. Suffering from my injuries and with no chance of healing or restoring myself.

And it was all over at the hands of my sick, twisted, demonic father, and I couldn't even open my mouth to scream.

"It's almost time," he said, pressing the blade above my shoulder joint, "so I'll make this quick. You can thank me for that later."

I didn't feel the blade as he sliced in, but I did hear the loud grunt as he fell backward, suddenly off balance. And though I couldn't turn my head, I was at the perfect angle to see why—the blade protruding from Rachel's chest. Just to the left of her heart.

She gasped and grabbed for it, yanking it out and snarling as Rose raced forward, slowing only long enough to take my blade from my thigh holster.

"You son of a bitch," she said, kicking out and catching Johnson under the chin. "You used me. You *raped* me. And Lily." She spun around, her heel knocking him solid across the face. "You've been playing with her like a damn puppet. Our whole family. Well, *no more*."

She kicked, and Johnson tumbled backward, then climbed to his feet, clearly not yet comfortable enough in the body to have his fighting game down.

But he did have a knife, and he lunged at Rose. She shifted left, evading, then lashed out with another kick. I wanted to cry out to her, to scream that she needed to finish the job, not vent her frustrations, but I was frozen, helpless, and could only watch as Rose was finally able to get her revenge against Lucas.

And it was some nasty revenge. She was a woman

on fire, fury driving her, Johnson barely even able to get in a decent thrust.

"I hate you," she said, the simple words carrying so much meaning. "I hate you, and you are dead." And with that, she slammed my knife into his heart, then pried her own knife from his weakening hand. She thrust it in, too, and when he fell back to the ground, she shoved it the rest of the way with her foot.

And then, as the body started to turn to goo, she pulled out the knives and spat on him.

Honestly, I wanted to applaud.

Rose stood gasping for breath, her expression a mixture of pride and amazement. Then she looked at me, and worry flooded her eyes. She crouched beside me. "Oh God, oh God. She died—she must have truly died—and he slid in to use her body. And then you healed him, and, oh God, he's been using her body ever since, and Rachel's been gone, and we never even knew." She licked her lips, tears spilling from her eyes. "We never even knew."

Tears spilled down her cheeks, and as Rose lifted my hand and sliced my wrist, the world faded away, and I was gone, too.

TWENTY

"*Come on! Come on! We have to hurry! Come on!*"

I woke up to Rose's face above mine, and the taste of blood lingering in my mouth. *My blood.* I blinked and sputtered and slowly, painfully, drew in a deep breath.

"Johnson?" I managed, my voice sounding croaky and off. "He's really dead? I didn't imagine it?"

Rose nodded, busying herself with pushing me into a sitting position, but when she looked up at me, I saw pain in her eyes. "He raped me," she said. "He tormented me and he hurt me and he raped me. But when I killed him, he was—" Her gaze darted over to the greasy stain on the floor.

"It wasn't Rachel anymore," I said gently. "And you killed the son of a bitch who was abusing her body. Who'd abused you. I say congrats and good riddance."

And, I thought, of all the ways that this could have turned out, having Rose actually destroy the man who'd fucked with her for so long was some serious poetic justice.

"Are you mad?"

I experimentally tried to move my legs and was pleased to see they were cooperating. "About what?"

"Who he was. What he did to you. Maybe you wanted to kill him."

I almost laughed. Because as much as that would have been a nice warm, fuzzy moment for me, the last thing in the world I wanted was to absorb the essence of Lucas Johnson. "No," I said. "I'm not mad. I am worried, though. How long was I out?"

"Only a minute or so," Rose said. "I wasn't sure how long it would last, so I tried the blood thing since you use it to heal folks, and, oh, Lily, we really need to hurry. The demons—"

"What about them?"

"She only did a protection on the front. On the back of the pub, she did an invitation. Or he. At any rate they're coming in. I got a few when I was coming up the stairs but Deacon's down there all alone, and he's helpless and—"

"*What?*" Deacon and helpless used together in the same sentence really didn't compute.

"The same stuff that got you," Rose said. "Only Rachel—I mean Johnson—was aiming it at me. He said he was done with me, and that it would end me slowly, and I'd probably last just long enough to hear you scream when he took the key from you. And then he was aiming this thing at me, like a blowgun or something, and Deacon jumped, and he was in front of me, and the dart got him instead of me. And I guess Johnson didn't want to try again, and so he turned and ran."

"Deacon?"

"It was working slower on him than it did on you—I guess because he's a demon and all—but he told me to go. To help you. And so I did, and on the way all these demons were coming in—like five—and Johnson saw one grab me, and that was when he told me what he'd done. The invitation, I mean. And then he went into the apartment, and I know he figured that the demon would kill me, you know?"

"But you nailed its ass."

"Yes, I did," she said, with a proud lift of her chin. "That one and the other four, too."

"What?"

She lifted a shoulder. "They all came to help it, but I got them. I had my blade and I had two more knives in my belt that I'd taken from the kitchen, and I was wearing your sword, too, 'cause I was practicing with it." She shrugged. "That meant I had to kill one by hand, but that was okay because—"

"Wow," I said.

She grinned, and any shadow of the pain from killing Johnson faded. "You're impressed. You're, like, really impressed."

I couldn't deny it. "Come on." I was still a little

wobbly, but I was moving, and at the moment I couldn't ask for much better than that.

On the stairs, I saw the corpse of one of the demons she'd killed—not with her blade, though. This one had his neck broken. Apparently my little sister really had graduated to über-chick rank.

"Let's make sure he stays dead, shall we?" I asked, and before the words were even out of my mouth, Rose pulled her blade and shoved it smack into the demon's heart.

"Better?"

"Hell, yes," I said, referring to both the kill and my little sister's confidence. A whole new persona to go with her new body. I had a partner again, a woman who'd survived and thrived. And even though a part of me mourned the loss of the little sister I'd worked so hard to take care of, another part of me rejoiced at having a sister who was confident and whole and didn't need to be coddled.

I'd told my mom I'd look after her, and I think that maybe—just maybe—despite all the weirdness, my mom would be pleased with the way Rose turned out. Somehow, someway, despite all my fumblings, I really had managed to save my baby sister.

I stepped over another demon carcass and peered around the corner. Nothing.

"I think we may be safe."

"Why would they stop coming in?" Rose asked.

I didn't have an answer to that. "Maybe they realized what a badass you are."

She rolled her eyes. "Or maybe there's someplace else they want to be."

"Or there's some reason to avoid here," I said, as the ground started to shake beneath my feet. *"Run."* And with Rose at my heels, we raced through the stone corridor, through the kitchen, and into the pub's public area, the floor behind us bursting up as the demon below raced after us, ripping up the wooden floor as he traveled.

Deacon lay sprawled on the ground near the bar, and my chest constricted with fear. An owned blade was the only thing that could truly kill a demon and prevent its essence from coming back in another form, but a mortal wound could kill the body, and I was terrified that if Deacon had died, this was the end of the man I needed. That I loved.

"Is he?"

"I don't know," I said, racing forward. "You said it worked slower on him?"

"I don't know how much," she said, then looked behind her at the rising, rippling floorboards. "It's getting closer. Lily, *Lily*, it's getting closer!"

"Grab him," I said, grabbing him under one arm while Rose got the other. We hauled him toward the front door, and while we did, I held my free hand out for Rose. "Cut."

She didn't hesitate, just sliced at the pad of my thumb. Blood oozed out, and I shoved my hand toward his mouth as we dragged his body toward the door. So far, he hadn't moved, but I refused to give up hope.

"Get the door," I shouted, as a giant tentacle lashed up through the ground.

Penemue, I thought. Either that or he and Kokbiel looked an awful lot alike. Then again, what did I know?

While Rose held the door open, I yanked Deacon through and into the street.

The street, I saw, where at least half a dozen demons were clustered, their weapons drawn, their faces dark with anticipation.

Fuck.

And then, Deacon stirred.

I exhaled, so relieved I wanted to cry. Unfortunately, I really didn't have the time. This definitely qualified as one bright spot in an otherwise completely fucked-up situation. "Drink more," I said, keeping my wound to his mouth. He sucked, the sensation curling through me like a hot wire, and as I knelt beside him, I held on to his shoulder for strength.

"Here's the situation. I've got the dagger, but we've got six demons on the street behind us. Penemue's about to burst through that door any minute. And we're an hour away from the convergence. We need to get out of here and get to the bridge. Can you fight?"

"Fight now; recover later," he said, climbing to his feet. And, I noticed, he didn't look nearly as shaky as I had. I might have special healing powers, but a bit of demon constitution was apparently a good thing, too.

"That way," I said, nodding toward the six, who had now grown to eight. "We get past them, we get a car, and we get the hell out of here."

I might be our general, but that was as specific as I had the time or the inclination to be. And it turned out my little speech was just the right length, too, because right as I finished it—right as we were racing forward, weapons drawn, ready to hack away at the growing mob—Penemue emerged.

No, strike that. He didn't emerge. He exploded. He ripped his way out of the bowels of the earth, sending asphalt and glass and all sorts of debris raining down on us.

The size of a semitruck, Penemue filled the street, his bulbous, tentacled body spreading out like a disease over the earth. Maggots crawled over his rotted flesh, and the stench that rose from him was enough to make me puke. Four squidlike tentacles curled around him, ready to lash out, just waiting for a victim to make a false move. The soulless eyes, black and beady, focused on me, and vomit yellow slime dripped from an orifice that might or might not be a nose.

He was horrible and huge and desperately dangerous.

He was evil.

And he wanted me.

"Playtime is over," he said, his voice filling the street, probably filling the whole damn town. "You will give back what is mine or suffer."

Since I really didn't see an upside to cooperating with the beast, I didn't stop what I was doing. Which happened to be whaling on a pasty-faced demon brandishing a mace. Nasty business, a mace, but the sword Deacon tossed me courtesy of the demon he'd just beheaded was nasty, too, and I thrust up and twisted, capturing the flail and ripping the medieval weapon right out of his hands. I didn't waste time recovering the mace; I just let go, grabbed my own blade, and lunged forward, catching the demon hard and fast in the gut.

His eyes widened, as if he was really astounded I'd done that, then he fell forward and started melting away.

One down, an entire mob of apocalyptic demons to go.

At least it was a start.

"Lily! Behind you!"

I turned to find a demon racing toward me, his knife outstretched. I started to dive left, but the demon's voice—"SHE IS MINE"—rushed over both of us, and my attacking demon dropped his knife, bowed, and turned tail to race in the other direction.

I thought that running thing was a damn fine idea, and decided to try it myself, but didn't have nearly the same success as my now-absent attacker. Because instead of running forward, I was being sucked backward.

"Lily!" Deacon yelled as I was dragged through the air as if I were being sucked into a black hole. "Vortex!"

I grabbed the first thing I passed—a lamppost—and clutched my fingers tight around it. In front of me, Deacon lunged in my direction, only to be brought back into the fight by two demons intent on not letting him get to me. Rose had similar problems, but at least she was holding her own. I hoped she could keep it up.

At the moment, there wasn't a damn thing I could do but hold on.

I tightened my grip and looked over my shoulder, then immediately wished I hadn't. Because what I saw was damn scary.

What I saw was like a huge black hole. A portal to somewhere far, far away.

"You possess what you do not own," Penemue said. "Return what is mine, and I will spare you."

I was really not buying that. And even if I did, I wasn't about to hand over the damn thing.

I expected him to rush forward and rip it from my neck, and when he didn't, it took a moment for me to realize why—he hadn't yet fully emerged into this dimension. He was stuck in one place. Which, normally, would make me happy. But considering he seemed more than capable of making me come to him, I have to say the situation was hardly ideal.

"It is mine," he boomed. "I created it. I imbued it with the power you would exploit. You know this," he said. "And the *Oris Clef* knows it as well."

For the first time I realized that the necklace was not simply stretched straight out toward the vortex like I was. Instead, it was twisting. Slowly. Subtly. But soon it would twist tight enough to choke me. Tight enough, possibly, to cut through the flesh in my neck.

And since the chain was demon-forged, I had to assume it could slice through bone, muscle, and tendons, too.

"It will be mine again," Penemue said. "One way or the other."

I called out for Deacon again, only to realize that the horde had increased at least twofold, and more demons were on their way. He and Rose were back-to-back and fighting for all they were worth. They were holding their own, but they couldn't be any help to me.

I was trapped. And if I didn't figure out what to do soon, Penemue would be the new king of the world.

Really not my idea of a sympathetic monarch.

The tug on my body increased, and I realized that the vortex was becoming more powerful. A trash can beside me tumbled and rolled, then leaped into the air and flew backward, and I twisted my head to watch, the muscles in my arms straining as I held tight to my lamppost. It rocketed toward the maw and never even slowed. Just got sucked in like something out of a fifties sci-fi flick featuring the black hole that ate Cincinnati.

Nothing past where the trash can had been, though, seemed to be affected, and I had to assume that Penemue had set the point of no return for the vortex at my lamppost. Everything past the lamppost was going about its business. Everything inside—like me and the *Oris Clef*—were feeling one hell of a brutal tug.

I strained to hold on, but it was getting harder and harder. The pull was unbelievably fierce, my entire body stretched out so much I was pretty sure that at the end, I'd be two inches taller.

"You cannot win, little girl." The voice, like sandpaper soaked in brine, grated on me, giving me chills.

"The hell I can't," I said. "I let go, and me and this necklace are slamming straight into your vortex. I don't know where it goes, but I'm guessing you won't be able to get us back in time to use the *Oris Clef* at the convergence."

"Such naïve innocence," he said. "Do you even now not understand? Do you not see why the elements of the *Oris Clef* appeared on your skin? Why you were able to track them down? Because it is bound to this dimension, Lily. It is bound here, as you are not."

Honestly, I didn't completely understand what he was talking about, but I definitely understood that whatever it was, it was bad for me.

"You will be drawn in, but the necklace will not. It will be plucked off your pretty neck and fall here, to the ground, at my feet."

That wasn't good. And what was worse was the fact that the world was starting to get very fuzzy, and I wasn't entirely sure why. Because my head wasn't working right anymore. Because the necklace had managed to twist itself around, and although I was an über-chick, I still need to breathe.

And that was becoming really, really hard.

And so was holding on to the damn post . . .

I blinked, my body jerking and my hands tightening. Through the sheer force of will, I was going to stay conscious, but I didn't have long. And I couldn't even cry out for Deacon—not that he could break away from his own personal war zone—but even if he could, my voice didn't seem to be working.

I was fast approaching the end, and I didn't like the way it looked. Didn't like it at all, and in less than an hour, the demons would cross over, and this would all be really and truly over.

No.

There had to be help somewhere. But I couldn't think where. Morwain was gone, and for the first time I truly appreciated how handy a minion could be. But while there might be other demons out there supporting me, none had bothered to tell me, and I didn't know them and couldn't call them if I did, and as my head spun and the world shifted from clear to gray to red, I did something I hadn't done in ages and ages.

I prayed.

I prayed for help. For strength. For God to me to show me the way to battle this demon because without help, it was all over. For me and for everybody else.

And when I was finished praying I opened my eyes and the world was still red and my fingers were still straining and I had no answers, and that tiny flower of faith that had been growing inside me started to shrivel up and die, the petals falling off and drifting away just like my crazy, oxygen-starved thoughts, and—

Gabriel.

Suddenly he was there. Not the angel, but the thought of him. Because *he* could save me. I had no doubt about that. And I knew he was near—knew he could come. I'd seen him all around me. In the face of that man at the church. In Madame Parrish. Inside the pages of the book. He'd been watching my every step, and he had to know that I hadn't failed. I'd found the key.

Now I just needed help getting to the bridge in time to use it.

I couldn't scream to call for him, though, and so I prayed some more, hoping that once again my prayers would be heard.

"Do you finally understand?"

I opened my eyes and saw him standing just behind the lamppost, unaffected by the vortex.

"Do you understand?" he repeated.

I understand you have to help me, I screamed inside my head. *If he gets the Oris Clef . . .*

"You will come with me? Willingly? You will come to the bridge?"

Fear curled in my gut. *I don't have to,* I said, then rushed on as I saw destruction rise in his countenance. *We found the third key. We can shut the gate. I don't have to burn. I don't have to be queen. It's over—or it will be if you help me. Please, Gabriel, on all that is holy. Help me.*

He took a single step toward me, his furrowed brow making the warrior tats on his face writhe and jump. "The third key. You speak the truth?"

Right there, I said, indicating the belt loop of my jeans through which I'd shoved the thing.

Storm clouds gathered in his eyes, as if he feared that I was trying to bullshit him.

Dammit, if he gets me, it's all over for you anyway, third key or not! Do you think you could find me in time? Pull me out of a portal to God knows where in time to stop hell from rushing toward us?

"ENOUGH," boomed Penemue. "This puny celestial creature is no match for me."

And to prove it, he yanked, and yanked hard. So hard I feared my arms would be pulled off.

"Lily!" Rose yelled, but I couldn't look up, couldn't answer. All I could do was try to hold on, and even that was no use, because as my fingers were starting to slip, the damn lamppost was being yanked from the ground.

I was hurtling toward the void, and there wasn't a damn thing I could do about it.

"No." Gabriel's voice echoed through Boston, and faster than I could comprehend, he whipped past me, his form no longer human, but celestial, a huge, dragonlike creature daubed with silver, both terrifying and beautiful. I caught only a glimpse as he burst past, but I heard the collision as he intercepted Penemue.

For that matter, I'm pretty sure Beijing heard the collision.

The world around us shook, the air itself shimmering like heat rising off concrete.

It was enough to shake me free, and I landed on the asphalt with a jolt, the pressure around my neck decreasing, and I tried desperately to claw at the ground and stop my still-backward progression to the maw.

In front of me, Rose tried to run to help, but she didn't make it. A demon attacked from behind, and she had to whip around and counter his blows. Soon, she was engulfed in a swarm, and though I called and called, I got no response.

I didn't see Deacon at all.

I tried to hold on and twist around, but I couldn't. I could only turn my head and see, somewhat, the battle raging behind me. A battle that was tearing down buildings, ripping up concrete, and shaking the earth to its core.

And then I felt the *snap* and knew that Gabriel had pulled Penemue free from his dimension. The demon was fully in this world, which, frankly, I considered one hell of a mistake as that gave him an extra few inches of reach, and one of those nasty tentacles did just that—*reached* I mean. Right out to lash around my ankle and pull me, flailing, through the sky toward him.

I yanked my knife from my sheath and hacked at the thick flesh, but it was no use. We were coming closer and closer to the portal. Soon, it would be all over.

"Lily!" Gabriel's voice echoed down the street, and my mind tried to comprehend the size of him, the power of him.

He held up a glowing sword, as if pointing the tip to heaven. "I have faith, Lily. In the future," he said, his words so eerily familiar. "And in the choice you must make."

And with that, he brought down his sword onto the tentacle and sliced it off, causing me to crash to the ground. At the same time, he burst forward with supernatural speed, to crash into Penemue and send them both hurtling backward into the maw.

His voice echoed back to me as the vortex sealed itself. "Faith . . ."

And then they were gone.

And the clock was still ticking down.

TWENTY-ONE

*F*aith.

Gabriel's words hung in the air as I picked up speed, rushing down the street toward my sister and Deacon, still fighting their way through the mass of writhing demons.

Faith in my choices.

The familiar words flowed through me. Calming me and yet, at the same time, disturbing me.

I remembered now where I'd heard them before—at Madame Parrish's, when I'd had the vision. When I'd seen Gabriel's face on her body.

I shivered. Because how could he have faith in my choices when I didn't intend to make one? The third key saved me from that—let me hop-skip right over faith. It was the easy way out, and I'll wholeheartedly admit that I was glad that Deacon's faith in the key's existence had paid off.

Now we just had to use the thing. Which was easier said than done because we had to get our asses to the Zakim Bridge. And if we got there late, all bets were off.

"Deacon!" I shouted, sliding into the fray, my own blade in my right hand and the dagger in my left. "We have to get out of here!"

"All for that," he shouted back. "Got any ideas how?"

There were dozens of them still. Coming at us from all directions. I'd made my way to the middle, where Deacon and Rose stood back-to-back, and I joined in. We made a small circle of resistance, and though we were all strong—though I was certain we could hold out for one hell of a lot longer than your average Joe on the street—holding out wasn't what we needed.

We needed to actually *be* out.

"Got any bright ideas?" Rose said.

At my neck, the *Oris Clef* thrummed with power. Now that Penemue was gone, it had apparently decided that I was an okay mistress after all, and I could feel the warmth from it tingle through me. I didn't, however, feel supercharged. I couldn't hack through the crowd no matter how much I wanted to. I'd take down a hell of a lot of them, but I couldn't guarantee I'd get off that street alive.

And right then, I needed guarantees.

"Because if you do have one," Rose went on. "Now's the time."

I did have one, actually, but I hesitated to suggest it. Hesitated even to voice the possibility. But right then, we were all out of options, and I had to make the hard choices.

"Deacon," I said, hating myself for saying the words—for even thinking them—yet knowing that it was the only way. "Can you change? Can you fly us out of here?"

He didn't answer, and the silence cut me to the core. I felt small, as if I'd failed him. As if I'd failed us.

"If you ask me to do it," he said in a voice full of pain, "then I will."

I wanted to close my eyes and pray for strength, but the demons rampaging all around us prevented that luxury. My eyes stayed open, and my blade stayed active.

And, yes, I wanted to ask him to do it. But somehow the words wouldn't come. It felt too much like a betrayal, and I wasn't going to toss Deacon back to the wolves. Not when there was another way.

And I really hoped that there was another way.

"So we run for it," Rose said. "We count to three, and we just go. Fast as we can. That'll work, right?"

"Wrong," I said. "We might make it. Or we might end up dead."

I glanced quickly at her and saw her set her jaw. "I know the risks," she said. "I'm ready."

"Maybe you are," I countered, thrusting my blade out to nail a demon foolish enough to move in on his own. He fell back, dissolving in front of us, and as the sweet power filled me, I realized I'd reached up to hold the *Oris Clef* tight in my hand. Its power flowed through me. So sweet. So tempting. So—

"We can't do this much longer," Rose shouted, and Deacon yelled his agreement. All around us, the demons had moved in—swarming like flies who'd finally figured out the best way to attack a small group. They'd lose their advance team, but by the end of the battle, we'd be finished, and they'd be victorious. Not a great outcome for us and one I didn't intend to let happen.

"Stop!" I yelled, and the moment I did, I knew what I had to do.

I stepped away from Deacon and Rose, ignoring their cries of protest.

"Stop," I repeated, and this time my voice boomed out, as if it had been magically amplified. Because, apparently, it had. *"Let us pass."*

I waited, somehow knowing—absolutely knowing— that this would work, and yet still fearing that I was wrong.

I wasn't.

All of the demons that had rushed into the street now took a step back, their heads bowed. The ones right in front of us moved even farther back, actually getting down on their knees, so that by the time they were all done shifting about, there was what appeared to be a troop formation with a corridor right down the middle.

Wow.

I might not be queen yet, but I'd just had a taste of the power that went with the job, and I have to say, it was pretty damn sweet.

"Hurry," I said to Deacon and Rose. "It worked, but it may not stick."

"Holy shit," Rose said, as we raced down the street, then broke into the first car we found. "Holy freaking shit."

"About sums it up," I said, then turned to Deacon. "Can you get us to the bridge in time?"

According to the clock on the dash, we had less than forty minutes to get there.

Deacon grimaced. "No problem," he said, then gunned the thing. The bad news was that traffic was insane. The roads were a mess from the earthquakes and fires, and when Deacon slowed to take a corner, inevitably some idiot demon would toss himself on the car, thinking that would slow us down or something.

I didn't try the booming-voice routine again. Considering how fast Deacon was moving, I'd be long gone before any demon actually got the message.

"There!" I shouted, when we finally reached the entrance for the freeway that became the bridge. "Faster! Faster!"

Deacon didn't answer, just kept barreling forward as time ticked away until we finally came to a screeching halt just at the edge of the Charles River. Close, but not exactly where we needed to be.

We couldn't, however, get to where we needed to be because of the cars that were practically stacked on one another in what had to be the worst traffic jam I'd ever seen.

"Eight minutes," Deacon said with an accusing glance toward the clock. "We need to run."

Also not easy with all those cars, but we managed, scrambling around and over until we reached the first tower that stretched up into the sky, the cables draping down to form an angel's wing.

"What now?" I asked Deacon. Beneath us, the bridge started to sway, and the water of the Charles started to bubble. The bright daytime sky started to fade, the shadow of the moon falling across the sun. An eclipse. And not one that scientists had predicted. This eclipse was all about portents and portals and heralding doom.

"What's happening?" Rose asked, grabbing onto one of the cables. Around us, civilians gaped, although we weren't attracting as much attention as we would have had it not been the end of the world. After all, the boiling river was at least as interesting as the crazy, knife-wielding people standing on top of the stalled cars.

"Demon coming," I said, nodding toward the water. And then with a tilt up to the sky. "And a whole lot more after that."

"Up," Deacon said. "We need to climb up."

We started to climb, which was not exactly an easy feat, as the cables were slick and set at an impossible angle. It's times like that when superstrength really does come in handy, and although I won't say we scaled the cables with ease, we did manage to make it to the top. Or I did. Deacon was close behind me, and Rose was taking up the rear, hanging on with one hand and battling back a wiry, fuzz-covered demon that had followed her up.

I had a similar problem, because when I reached the top of the concrete tower, I found myself sharing my tiny little chunk of concrete with a snarling, snapping monkey-shaped demon who had apparently come up on the opposite set of cables, just to piss me off.

"It's coming," Deacon said. "Lily, it's rising!"

Rising?

I risked a sideways glance and saw that the portal was indeed rising. A sliver of dark, like a cat's pupil, had formed out of thin air, a few feet above the river. As it rose, it expanded, and from what Deacon had said about the portal opening above the towers, I figured it would be wide enough for hell to burst through by the time it got up here.

"What do I do?" I said. "How do I use the key?"

The dagger had come with no instructions, no nothing, and the portal was not shaped like a giant keyhole, nor did it resemble a bull's-eye where the knife should hit dead center.

"Shove the knife in," Rose called up. "Before it gets too big."

Since that sounded like as good a plan as any, I started to shinny back down the cables, wanting to position myself above a relatively small portal rather than a gaping maw.

The demon sharing the tower with me wasn't keen on the idea of my leaving, though, and he lunged toward me. I shifted, lost my balance, and started to fall off the tower. I reached out to balance myself, and ended up grabbing the serrated edge of his knife and ripping my hand to shreds.

The blood made my hand slick as I reached down to grab the cables, but I had a decent enough grip, and I used it to steady myself as I lashed up with my leg, whipped it sideways, and sent him tumbling off the tower into space.

I shifted my grip and slid down the cable, and this time the blood on my hand turned out to be pretty useful, as it got the cable all slippery and increased the speed of my downward shinny at least threefold.

I stopped when the portal was about a foot below me. About the size of the mouth of a jar of pickles, and I thrust out and stabbed the blade hard into the rising void, then held my breath anticipating—something. A *whoosh*ing sound, maybe, as the portal slammed shut.

There was, however, no whooshing.

There was, in fact, no nothing.

Worse, the portal was still rising, and all of a sudden I was actually below the damn thing.

Shit.

I shifted the knife to my bloody hand, then shoved it in my belt again as I climbed yet again up the cables, calling down to Deacon as I went. "It didn't work! What did I do wrong?"

He, however, didn't answer, as he was otherwise preoccupied fighting off the five demons that had managed to climb up and surround him as he clung with one hand to a cable and tried to battle them off with the other.

I reached the top of the tower, thankfully faster than the portal, which was growing bigger. I could hear them, the waiting demons, biding their time until the portal opened.

And around my neck, the *Oris Clef* seemed to sing, trying to draw me in, to entice me, to pull me toward the dark.

I thought about what it could do for me. The power I could wield.

No. Not power. Good. The good I could do. The control I could foist upon the demons, just as I had made them bow down to me during our escape. It had felt right, that power. I could do that.

I could.

And because the third key didn't work, there really was no other way.

Or, rather, the only remaining way still made me quiver with fear, especially since the portal was still widening, and I could peer down. Especially when I could see the writhing shadows of the hordes and feel the rising heat of the hellfire.

Especially having felt the power of what I would be giving up.

I swallowed, calling on my courage. I could do this—I could lead, and so I lifted my hand high, then raised the dagger that was still in my hand. My palm was already bloody, but in the vision, I'd sliced my hand right before grasping the *Oris Clef*, and now was not the moment to veer from procedure.

Beneath me, I could hear Rose and Deacon battling fiercely as demons climbed up the cables beneath them.

I drew in my breath, then issued a command, just as I had on the street. "Stop!" I cried, but this time there was no booming undertone, and the demons did not even hesitate.

I understood why—the *Oris Clef* had given me a taste of power. But now, for more, I had to fully embrace my throne.

Rose's scream pierced my ear, and I looked down, saw that the sharp talon of a demon's claw had ripped into her thigh. It was bleeding badly, the wound exposed all the way down to the bone, and my sister's face was pale, her breathing shallow, though she was still fighting, still holding her own.

I clutched the dagger tighter. I had to do this. One moment. One change, and I could save Rose.

I brought the dagger toward me—then stopped.

My blood was smeared on the blade, and I saw that the blood had raised an inscription. *For my daughter. May you find the courage to do what must be done.*

My heart stuttered in my chest, and I felt tears prick my eyes. Margaret had believed it would be her own daughter, Alice, who stood on this precipice, but the words seemed meant only for me.

I understood now the real truth—why I'd been unable to locate the dagger in the book. Not because it was in another dimension, but because I'd been searching for the key. And the dagger was not a key; it couldn't close the gate. It couldn't prevent the Apocalypse.

Instead, it was a gift. A mother's gift to the daughter she believed would save the world.

Oh God.

Beneath me, the portal gained speed, rising faster and faster. I stood there, torn and terrified. The time to make a decision was now, and I was paralyzed.

That, however, didn't last for long, as I was thrown into motion when the bridge began to buckle.

The screams of the humans on the bridge reached my ears, along with the cry of my sister. "The water. Lily, look at the water!"

I looked, and as it bubbled and hissed—as the bridge shook with tremors—something large and gray was rising to the surface.

A violent jolt shook my tower, and I fell to my stomach, grasping one of the cables as I tried to ride out the waves. Beneath me, I watched with horror as the bridge split down the middle, the concrete breaking, the steel cables snapping. Cars and people tumbled into the river, their screams drowned out by the screech of ripping metal and the roar of shattering concrete.

Rose, too, went down, and it was my turn to scream as she fell, then even louder when I saw what caught her—a hideous beast emerging from the bubbling, steaming river that was slowly evaporating, dissipated by the hellish heat generated by a massive demon that could only be Kokbiel.

That is right, little bitch. I am Kokbiel. I am the destruction and the light. I am your origin and your destiny. I am the one who will rip the head off this foolish child if you do not give me what I want.

The Oris Clef, *my child.*

Give it to me, and I will let you rule at my side, your sister a princess, your male a prince.

Give it to me, and fulfill your destiny as my heir, for my blood—my essence—burns in your veins. Of this, you already know.

Give it to me, he said. *And together we can transform the world.*

TWENTY-TWO

I clutched the *Oris Clef* tight.

No way, *no way in hell*, was I giving it to a demon like Kokbiel.

But I had to save Rose. I had to do something, and I had to do it fast, or else I'd lose not only Rose but the whole damn world.

I looked down to gauge the location of the portal, and realized that it was no longer beneath me. The quake that had shaken the tower had also lowered it—and shoved it down so that it was now at an angle to the riverbed, whereas before it had been perpendicular. Instead of the portal being a straight drop below me, it was not only above me but also about twenty feet away.

Which meant that unless I could sprout wings and fly, I wasn't doing a single damn thing. Not the *Oris Clef*, not my own sacrifice, not anything.

Closing the gate meant being *at* the gate, and I couldn't get there.

Kokbiel, rising up to stretch out wings beneath me, though . . .

Well, I could see that he wasn't going to have similar problems. More than that, I knew what was going to happen, and I braced myself for another earthquake—the final one, which would shake him free of the dimension from which he was emerging.

And once he was out, he would rise up, straight to me.

Straight for the *Oris Clef* I wore around my neck.

Now, girl. The child's time is running out.

He had Rose tight around the chest, and her face was pale as she gasped, trying to draw breath. But she didn't scream. She didn't cry. She just looked up at me with pleading, defiant eyes, and mouthed the word, "No."

Screw this.

I knew what I had to do, and I scanned the area beneath me for Deacon. He was on a bobbing piece of concrete, the cable he'd been clinging to apparently having snapped. He balanced on it like a life raft as he cut down demon after demon trying to capsize him and thrust him into the boiling water.

"Deacon," I shouted. *"Fly."*

He looked up at me, confused, as if he couldn't have heard what he thought he had. As if he knew there was no way I would ask him to return to his demon state, because to even ask would be to betray everything between us.

I steeled myself, hating what I had to do, but knowing I had no choice. "Dammit, Deacon, you said you would change if I asked. Well, I'm asking now. I know what I have to do. But I need you to fly me."

"Lily, I—"

"Please." I could feel the tears clogging my throat. "Deacon, trust me. I need you to trust me."

He hesitated, then bowed his head. And when he looked up again, I saw fire in his eyes, along with self-loathing and a desperate control.

I also saw his wings, spreading out, strong and powerful. He rose, a majestic beast clinging to a frayed thread of control, and rushed straight toward me.

"Where?" he growled.

"Take me," I said, hoping my gamble would pay off. Hoping that the demon inside him wouldn't burst out and control the man. It was a horrible risk I was taking. He could rip me apart and toss my limbs into the boiling water. He could take the *Oris Clef* from me.

He could do any damn thing he wanted because once he had grabbed me under the arms and lifted me, I would be dangling below him, helpless.

"Hurry," I shouted.

Below, Kokbiel was rising out of the water, Rose still clutched in a tentacle, but apparently not his main concern. *That*, I was pleased to see, was now me.

Another violent shudder of the earth, and Kokbiel burst free, flying up toward us with an impossible wingspan, my sister still tight in his grip.

"Take me!" I yelled again. "Dammit, Deacon, go!"

He did, grabbing me and shooting forward, Kokbiel hot on our heels.

Deacon put on a burst of speed, and—*yes*—we were over the portal, looking down at the maw and at the horsemen that were now barreling down the long, interdimensional corridor toward the now-open gate.

"Let go," I cried. "Drop me."

But he didn't, his rough refusal costing us precious seconds. "Lily, I can't."

Kokbiel reached us, grabbing Deacon's leg and jerking us back just far enough that we were no longer over the portal.

"Deacon, I have to. You have to trust me. Please, please, get us back."

But he couldn't. He was moving in the opposite direction. He was simply no match for Kokbiel, not as he was, still fighting his demon side.

I heard a roar and realized it came from him, followed by a blast of fire. *He'd changed.*

Deacon had taken on the full mantle of his demon, and with a burst of fire and speed, he broke free of Kokbiel.

He was a demon, though. Brother to those who were crossing. And I could only hope that there was still enough Deacon in him to do what had to be done.

He rose, away from the portal, and I grabbed my blade tighter, fearing I would have to thrust it upward, into his heart. Fearing I'd have to try—somehow—to nosedive through space and into the widening portal before it was too late.

But then, just when I feared the worst, he dropped me, and as his guttural howl meshed with Rose's sharp-pitched scream, I fell down, down, down into the waiting mouth of hell.

Into the choice I had to make right then.

I didn't know if I could save Deacon, or if I could once again save my sister. But I did know that I could save the world. And that, I thought, was something.

Around my neck the *Oris Clef* tightened, and then the chain snapped, the master key falling fast toward the boiling water, bound to this dimension while I plummeted toward hell.

Then, with my sister's cries echoing in my ears, I brought Alice's dagger to my breast, and plunged it in.

The blade slid through my flesh, and my blood poured into the portal. And as I fell toward the suffering that awaited me, I finally understood: That was what the dagger had been meant for all along. In a way, it really was the missing key. But it was useless without me.

TWENTY-THREE

"*You did well, Lily. You made the sacrifice willingly, even knowing the price you would pay.*"

"*There was no other choice to make.*"

"*There was. But you had faith. Faith in your choice and in your courage. And faith, Lily, has its own rewards.*"

"*I don't understand.*"

"*You will. Good-bye, Lily Carlyle. We will meet again.*"

Nothing.

Not black. Not white. Not color or light.

Just . . . nothing.

No fiery pit. No burning flesh. No anything.

And then the softest hint of a breeze, the wind upon tender flesh. The scent of flowers. The cool crush of grass beneath my cheek.

Grass?

I wiggled my fingers experimentally. That certainly felt like grass. My toes followed suit and came up with the same conclusion. Running out of options, I gathered my courage, then opened my eyes fast. One quick peek.

And I liked what I saw.

I opened them a little wider. Grass, all right.

I shifted, rolling over so that my back was on the grass and the sky would be above me. Blue, with fluffy white clouds.

I smiled.

Under the circumstances, this was rather unexpected.

Almost as unexpected as the man who stepped up, shirtless, his face blocking the sun and shadowing me, his smile warming me.

"Where am I?"

Deacon reached down to give me his hand. I took it, letting him pull me up and guide me into his arms. "You did it."

I swallowed. "I closed the gate?" I glanced around, confused, a jumble of images and emotions, of fear and fascination, pounding inside my mind. "Then it was real," I said with wonder. "What I heard? What Gabriel said?"

"I don't know what he said," Deacon said. "All I know is that you stopped the horde. You saved the world, Lily." He stroked my cheek. "And then you came back."

"Rose?"

His smile was soft and understanding. "You saved

her, too." He nodded to a figure in the distance, hurrying toward us over the cool park grass. "The force of the gate slamming shut weakened Kokbiel. He's not dead, but he's gone for now."

I closed my eyes in a silent prayer. I'd gambled, but this time it had turned out right. Rose was safe. Deacon was back. And the world, for now, was safe.

"You made the right choice, Lily," Deacon said. "We both did."

"I can't believe it," I said, as my sister launched herself into my arms, her leg bandaged with Deacon's ripped-up shirt.

"You're alive," she said. "We did it, and you're alive."

Tears were streaming down her face. I brushed them away, then realized she was doing the same to me.

"It's over," I whispered, hooking one arm around Rose's waist and reaching out my hand for Deacon. "I can't believe it's really over."

Deacon and Rose exchanged a glance.

"It's not over?"

"You closed the gate, Lily," Deacon said, "and the world's going to keep on turning. But there are still demons here. Still portals that can be opened. Still evil in the world."

"And somebody has to kill the demons," Rose said, her hand going automatically to her knife.

I nodded, understanding. Some of that evil still lived within me. I could feel it inside, struggling to get out. But I finally knew that I was strong. Strong enough to make the hard choices. The *right* choices.

If there was still evil in the world, I'd step up to the plate and fight it. I could be über-girl-assassin-chick. I could control the demons—the ones in the world and the ones that lived inside me.

And with Deacon and Rose at my side, we could seriously kick Evil's butt. I was even looking forward to it.

Right then, though?

Right then, I was taking the night off.

Honestly, I think I deserved it.

M529T0709

DON'T MISS THE SECOND BOOK IN THE
BLOOD LILY CHRONICLES
FROM *USA Today* BESTSELLING AUTHOR
JULIE KENNER

TORN

Lily is in trouble of the deepest kind. Having been tricked
by the forces of evil, she killed what she thought were
"demons." Now she knows better, and with a little help
from half angel, half demon Deacon Camphire, she must
try to take down the bad guys from within as a double
agent.

NOW AVAILABLE FROM ACE BOOKS!

**Explore the outer reaches
of imagination—don't miss these authors
of dark fantasy and urban noir that take you
to the edge and beyond.**

Patricia Briggs	Karen Chance	Anne Bishop
Simon R. Green	Caitlin R. Kiernan	Janine Cross
Jim Butcher	Rachel Caine	Sarah Monette
Kat Richardson	Glen Cook	Douglas Clegg

penguin.com

M15G0907